MRS ROBINSON

Zillah's catering business, *Mrs Robinson*, provides fabulous wedding and party food in beautiful Bath. After newcomer Hal Christmas rents the neighbouring offices — and steals her trading name! — the two manage to move from insults to compromise. Neither one acknowledges the electricity growing between them, but Hal becomes grumpy when financial strain obliges Zillah to share her flat with his charming and roguish friend Zak. Until, that is, an accident allows Zillah the opportunity to reveal her soft heart . . .

JILL BARRY

◆

MRS ROBINSON

Complete and Unabridged

LINFORD
Leicester

First published in Great Britain in 2016

First Linford Edition
published 2016

A catalogue record for this book is available
from the British Library.

ISBN 978–1–4448–2836–8

Published by
F. A. Thorpe (Publishing)
Anstey, Leicestershire

Set by Words & Graphics Ltd.
Anstey, Leicestershire
Printed and bound in Great Britain by
T. J. International Ltd., Padstow, Cornwall

This book is printed on acid-free paper

1

Zillah Robinson's office phone rang right in the middle of a fairy-dust-sprinkled fantasy. She was delivering a scrumptious four-course dinner to a glamorous movie star who had recently moved into a gorgeous Georgian mansion, high in the hills above beautiful Bath.

Just as he was smiling at her, she took the call. 'Mrs Robinson. How may I help?'

'I need a couple of hot singing waiters for a corporate function.' The woman's voice oozed confidence. It would be funny if only Zillah wasn't so desperate for business.

She suppressed a sigh, the fingers of one hand tapping on her keyboard. 'You're through to Mrs Robinson's gourmet catering service. I'm sorry we can't help with your entertainment query but we'd love to quote for your party food. Perhaps I could call with some menus?'

'The hotel we've booked is sorting out the catering.' The woman sounded impatient. 'Their functions manager advised me to call *Mrs Robinson* for singing waiters. Are you sure you can't help?'

'I'm sorry, but that's not my area of expertise. Perhaps someone has a warped sense of humour?' She smiled into the phone. 'So, may I take your contact details, please? I'd like to send you our brochure — email it if that's appropriate.'

Zillah scribbled down the information and gently replaced the receiver. The caller had actually asked her for the other Mrs Robinson's number. *Un-be-lievable*. This was the third peculiar enquiry in as many days. The first person wanted to book a serious singer for a country house hotel wedding. The second call was for a balloon-sculpting children's clown. She hadn't taken a single new booking this week for so much as a platter of cheese straws.

If the barbeque season coincided with sizzling weather or even a warm, dry spell, it usually blew impromptu business her way. Current conditions might suit mermaids but there weren't too many of those around. The only forward dates in Zillah's diary were wedding receptions. Thank goodness for romance — or even the triumph of hope over experience, given how many clients were marrying for the second time.

She stroked the silken patina of her desk, the elegant, walnut escritoire a poignant reminder of her past. Everything else bar her violet tweed office chair was white, even the floorboards. Her assistant Abi had sanded and painted them the year before, while Zillah pounded Bath's pavements, spreading the word round local businesses. Abi was a treasure, but with the firm about to blow out its first birthday cake candle, she remained unaware of how close to the rapids her boss paddled.

Zillah switched on the answerphone and headed for the kitchen. Opening the door, she stopped, obeying her own instruction: no way would she enter without her streaky honey-blonde hair tucked inside a hat. 'Abi,' she said, 'I really must check out this mistaken identity business. I've had enough of these odd calls.'

'What did they want this time?'

'Certainly not two hundred veggie samosas. Speaking of which?'

'All under control, boss, and I've set the timer for the beef sirloin. Will you be long?'

'As long as it takes to cross-examine our friendly pub landlord. Someone's taking my name in vain and I intend finding out who it is. Phone's taken care of and I shan't be long.'

★ ★ ★

Zillah, sheltering under a rainbow-striped golf umbrella, dodged puddles on the forecourt to reach her silver van. An access way linked the trading estate with the main Bath road, and her favourite inn straddled the city boundary. Nothing much happened in these parts without Mickey the landlord knowing — and if he didn't, he had ways of finding out.

She drove cautiously along the slip road. *Hell's teeth!* She was crawling in low gear, but did the black Jeep coming the other way intend conjoining with her wing mirror? She applied the brakes before jabbing the window button. The other vehicle burned rubber to stop. Its driver also opened his window.

'Didn't you see the sign?' Frowning, Zillah tucked a strand of hair behind one ear and pointed her finger. 'The one warning you not to exceed ten miles per hour?'

'Believe me, you were taking up half my side of the road.'

He sounded like a contemporary

equivalent of *Jane Eyre's* Mr Rochester on a very dark day. She tried to glare back, but found this difficult when longing to let her gaze roam. The man was arrogance personified, but his lips urged her to reach out a finger and trace their outline. The close-cropped, burnt-marmalade hair begged to be ruffled. A girl would feel safe in the shelter of those powerful arms. Capable hands, their tapering fingers with shapely, clean nails drumming the steering wheel, tapped into Zillah's thoughts so deeply that she felt the first stirrings of something she'd assumed lost forever.

The stranger craned his head through his window to assess the situation, scowled, but selected first gear. And shook his head, in exasperation. 'It's no good. You'll have to back up. Madam.'

'Why me?'

'Would you prefer me to do it for you?'

She swallowed. Attractive he might be, but he was clearly a misogynist toad. 'That's funny,' she said, 'I was about to offer the same to you.'

He stared back. She watched his lips twitch before he resumed his stern look. 'Look, I wonder if you can tell me whether these units are worth the rent the owner's asking. I'd really appreciate not wasting any more time. The one I'm considering is in the same block as the pine furniture store.' He shook his head again. 'I've already trawled the other half of this estate. Sign boards there are none.'

Zillah did her best to concentrate. The vacant unit on the floor above hers was under consideration by a couple running a soft-furnishing enterprise. They wanted to expand, but kept dithering. This good-looking guy, though pompous, must be another entrepreneur. The more firms on the business park, the more potential for her catering company. If Mr Bossy Boots decided to rent offices, he'd soon realise the speed restriction sign wasn't there to improve the scenery.

'I've no complaints,' she said. 'You'll find the furniture place at the end. The owner will show you round the vacant premises. There's only one unit left in that block.'

The man nodded. 'Thank you.'

He shifted gear and half-turned his body, one arm across the passenger-seat back, as he reversed to the point where Zillah could pass with confidence, although the tip of her tongue peeped between her cherry-glossed lips as she continued on her way.

If Hal hadn't been so intent upon trying to barter insults with the driver of the silver van, he might have noticed the words sign-written in shiny black on the side panel of her gleaming vehicle:

Mrs Robinson Ltd
Gourmet Catering

★ ★ ★

Zillah strolled into the bar of The Golden Fleece. 'May I have a filter coffee please, Jake?'

'It seems awful, having to charge you,' the young barman said as Zillah watched the machine hiss like a steampunk sideshow.

'Mickey has a business to run, Jake, exactly as I have. He's after a profit. And before you get your hopes up, I'm afraid I haven't come to book you for another function. You're still okay for Saturday, I hope?'

Jake placed a cup of black coffee on the counter. 'Of course I am. You know, once the weather settles, business will pick up. After all, it is summer.'

'I wish the weather realised that. To add to my gloom, some dope appears to be using my name.'

'Sorry?' Jake frowned. 'I'm not with you.'

'Sadly, I'm getting calls from people wanting to book cabaret turns; or, erm, burlesque dancers,' she said. 'You name it. When I gently point them in the direction of my food for the discerning, they say thanks, but no thanks.'

9

'That's really naff.'

'Yes,' she said. 'Because the hotel or golf club or whatever venue has scored the booking is taking care of the catering, and they've suggested ringing *Mrs Robinson* for a good time.'

He whistled. 'You want me to quiz the boss? He's in the cellar.'

Zillah's face relaxed. 'Please.' Jake was not only eye-candy. His IQ was on an intellectual level, and he was a good worker. But if anyone ever teased her about playing the movie role with her part-time employee, she swiftly put them right. Apart from the fact that he already had a girlfriend, Jake wasn't even twenty, while Zillah was . . . well, not quite as mature as the original Mrs Robinson; but that kind of stuff wasn't her style.

Jake didn't hang about. 'The guvnor says, leave it with him. He hasn't heard of any new business, but one of his mates works the graveyard shift at the Hilton Hotel. Mickey says this guy knows absolutely everything. When he wakes up, that is.'

★ ★ ★

Zillah drove back to work, cheered by a watery rainbow. She'd offloaded another pile of business cards at the pub because Mickey was sometimes asked to recommend a caterer. In her turn, Zillah always suggested The Golden Fleece if any clients required bed and mouth-watering breakfast without a staggering bill at the end.

Turning off, she negotiated the slip road at snail's speed; half-dreading, half-hoping to meet that obnoxious man again. She let herself into the building, absorbing the bouquet of slow-roasting beef and Northern Soul music drifting from the kitchen CD player.

'I'm back, Abi,' she called. 'I bought a couple of Mickey's pasties for our lunch. Too good to miss.'

'Did you get teased?'

'About avoiding our own cooking? Of

11

course. The main man emerged from the cellar, asking me to whip up something for his lunch.'

'He definitely has a soft spot for you.'

'I'm sorry?'

'Pity he's married. As well as ancient,' said Abi. 'I wonder if he really has three ex-wives, like they say.' She was pulling off her hat and white boots. 'Now — have I got news for you!'

'Someone viewed the vacant premises?'

Abi pouted. 'How did you guess?'

'A man almost drove into me.'

'So I don't need to tell you what a hottie he is?'

Zillah raised her hand. 'Believe me. You can't judge that particular book by its cover.'

Abi's expression was pitying. 'He was totally charming when he spoke to me. Of course, Hal's old, but not as ancient as Mickey. Now, better brace yourself.'

Zillah flopped into her chair. That chauvinist was 'old'? His name was Hal? Sometimes she forgot the divide

12

there was between twenty-two-year-old Abi and her thirty-six-year-old self.

'Just as well you sat down. Not only is the dreamboat going to rent the empty unit, he's starting an entertainments agency.' Abi paused for effect. 'Ta-da! Would you believe, he's the other *Mrs Robinson*.'

Zillah jumped to her feet. 'You're joking! Oh, please tell me you're joking, Abi.'

'I'm serious, boss.'

'But did he say he already knew about us? Surely he would've done his homework before choosing a name?'

'Dunno. He read the name board, that's why he knocked on our door. He seemed mildly surprised, but I think he's cool about it.'

'He is? That's big of him.'

Abi ignored her. 'Oh, and he said he'd already taken a couple of calls asking about catering, but didn't know who to recommend as he's still new to the area.'

Zillah sank into her seat again and

put her head in her hands.

'He's an accountant,' said Abi. 'He used to work for a big London partnership. I don't know why he relocated, but here he is. Wants to use local entertainers where possible, though he's got contacts that'll travel for the right fee. It sounds really exciting.'

'I'm so glad you enjoyed your chat. I might have known someone incapable of recognising a speed restriction sign wouldn't have the common sense to check out the name he chose for his new business.' Zillah wondered whether the situation demanded she take more caffeine on board.

Abi disguised a sharp intuition behind a ditzy exterior. 'I'll put the kettle on before I start washing salad vegetables for tomorrow.' She delved into her pinafore pocket. 'Here's Hal's business card. He said he's looking forward to meeting you. I'm sure you'll like him once you get to know him. I think he's cute.'

'About as cute as a piranha.' Zillah glanced at the card. Her lips curved in a slow smile. With a surname like his, surely he could have cashed in on it and come up with a company name that was really original?

2

Next morning in the van, Abi checked for text messages while she scolded her boss. 'It's not often a guy towers over *you*,' she said, as if Zillah was at least seven feet tall.

'I haven't seen him standing up.'

'Well, I have. And he's not wearing a wedding ring, plus there's no telltale pale mark, either.' She chuckled. 'Ooh, cool. Joe says he'll prepare a surprise for our lunch tomorrow, before he gets to the Nancarrow place this evening to help clear up.'

'You have a five-star boyfriend there, Abi.' Zillah followed her cross-country route, driving carefully — as you do when transporting luscious buffet food for one hundred.

'Mmm, I know. So when's your summit meeting? With the lovely Hal, I mean.'

16

'Mr Christmas and I are meeting on Monday afternoon.' Zillah's tone suggested pistols at dawn.

'Will he back down, do you think?'

Zillah's snort was unladylike. 'I doubt it. At the very least, I expect an explanation as to why he chose that name. It beggars belief.'

Abi pocketed her phone. 'My mum says there's something very evocative about 'Mrs Robinson'. It has a certain *je ne sais quoi*.'

'Good. I think so too, which is why I chose it. Apart from the fact that I have a legal right, considering it's mine by marriage. More importantly, *Mrs Robinson* is a registered limited company. It's *my* company, and your Hal is out of order.'

Abi ignored the gibe. 'With a name like his, he could've gone for something like *Jingles* or *Party Poppers*.'

'To be fair, I expect he's bored out of his skull with festive season jokes. What bugs me most is his not bothering to check out local businesses. I know

17

there's no copyright or anything like that. But he wouldn't have been allowed to set up a limited company of the same name. I mean, what gives with this man? Is he naïve or does he care nothing about other people?'

She paused, changed gear, and overtook a lumbering farm tractor pulling a trailer loaded with a pile of something she didn't care to think about. 'It's not my existing clients I worry about, because they check our website or ring to see what's on offer. It's new people who've found us by word of mouth that concern me. If they get hold of Hal Christmas by mistake and he tries to sell them a sword-swallowing act, what are they going to think?'

'I think you have to swallow your pride and get it on with this guy.'

'Over my dead body.'

'Whatever you might think about him, you'll have to get used to seeing him around the place.'

Zillah sighed.

'Two businesses will be run from the same building,' said Abi. 'There'll be two separate phone numbers. Surely the pair of you can cook up a plan?'

'And what plan would that be?'

'People who ring us wanting a troupe of high-kicking dancing girls — we give them Hal's number.' Abi hurried on. 'If anyone rings the wrong *Mrs Robinson*, wanting to book a chocolate fountain for a romantic novelists' knees-up — he gives them our number. It's not rocket science.'

Zillah wasn't convinced. 'It sounds all very well, but people easily lose interest once they're confused. Think about the older generation. They like things to be just so. I'll be condemned by association.' She slackened speed. 'The person who answers the phone can make or break. Worst scenario — his answerphone message, over which I have no control. You wait and see.'

Abi peered through her window. 'Wow, check out those cute pink balloons. Someone's making sure the guests don't overshoot the car park.'

They made slow progress as Zillah rounded a sharp bend. 'There's the driveway,' she said. 'On the positive side, this gig might turn out to be a goldmine for new clients. Could you reach my cards from the glove compartment, please? If we all have some tucked in our pockets, we can press them into people's hot little hands.' She glanced sideways at Abi. 'Only if they ask, of course.'

★ ★ ★

'Mrs Robinson, I can't thank you enough. I knew your standards were high, but the food has surpassed my wildest expectations. My husband and I would like you and your helpers to join us in the toast when we come to cutting the cake.'

'Thank you very much, Mrs Nancarrow. You and your family are a joy to deal with. If someone could be kind enough to let us know when you'd like us to fill the champagne flutes ready for the toasts — '

The bride's mother, sleek in coffee-coloured silk, beamed at Zillah. 'About twenty minutes from now. I'll go and speak to that delightful young barman of yours.'

She glided off in her matching lace court shoes towards the bar. Zillah, watching Jake turn into Tom Cruise, recognised the bride's mother's outfit as couture. She'd meant what she said to her. Such a warm compliment, when it happened, was always the glossy dark chocolate on the profiterole. Zillah was particularly pleased the family had chosen the bubbly she recommended. The medium-dry wine, with its hon-eyed buzz, was the perfect partner to a slice of rich, fruity wedding cake.

Zillah rated this reception an A-list one. The beautiful people, whether happy relatives or friends of bride and groom, said it all.

These celebrations weren't all the

same, of course. Sometimes, in spite of Zillah's almost military-like planning, the unexpected could detonate like a dented can of fizzy pop, peppering the whole affair with confusion. It could be a helper falling ill at the last moment. Or a guest who'd forgotten to mention their hen's-egg allergy.

Jake was eyeing her curiously. Zillah moved towards the bar.

'Everything okay?'

'Fine,' he said. 'Just wondered what you were smiling about.'

She chuckled. 'I was remembering something I'd prefer to forget. Tell you later. I'm off to find a ladies' room.'

Immaculate in her silver-grey short-sleeved dress and charcoal-and-white striped apron, Zillah headed upstairs. On discovering a door bearing a makeshift sign, she tapped discreetly. No one yelled. She found herself in a room big enough for a line-dancing session. It had to be the master bedroom, and it was a symphony of cream, gold and azure, the air sweet with the scent of lilies drifting from a crystal vase in the fireplace.

Sounds of someone in distress filtered from behind a door that had to lead to an en suite bathroom. Zillah almost backed out again. But the cobweb bridal headdress lying on the counterpane caught her eye. Its colour matched the gown — a cochineal drop in a dish of cream. Its fabric was shot with tiny slivers of silver, a fairytale veil for a bride whose own fairy story seemed hell-bent on trashing the traditional script.

She could either succeed in embarrassing herself, or might just possibly be able to help. Sometimes brides, too jumpy to eat enough to soak up the bubbly, let their imaginations convince them the groom still possessed warm feelings for an old flame displaying a cleavage capable of stunning a short-sighted vicar. On this occasion, instinct told her not to back off.

'Cara? It's Zillah Robinson. I'll go away if you say so.'

Silence. The bride probably regretted not securing the outer door. Zillah heard a tight little voice say, 'Yes, go away. No, don't! Sorry, Mrs Robinson — I'd like you to stay, please.'

'Shall I come in or will you come out?'

The door opened and Cara, surely bride of the year, emerged. But at that moment, she resembled, to Zillah's compassionate gaze, a lonely nine-year-old dressed up in her mother's wedding finery to enliven a dismal afternoon.

'Cold compress,' said Zillah briskly.

She shot through the bathroom door and cast her eye round. There was a pile of fluffy guest towels and linen napkins on a shelf. Why wouldn't there be? She chose the cloth that felt softest and held it under the cold tap before wringing it out and rejoining Cara.

'Here, hold this against your eyelids. I guess you're wearing waterproof mascara?' Maybe she'd been a little too hasty with her A-list wedding rating, but surely there was still time to repair the damage? Assuming Cara didn't plan on sliding down a drainpipe into the arms of the real man of her dreams, who stood poised to whisk her to a love nest in the Seychelles. But then, wouldn't she be changing into something less fragile than her bridal gown if she was about to do a runner?

Cara still sat on the end of the bed with Zillah perched next to her. The bride lowered the impromptu pink-eye reducer and managed an almost-there smile. To Zillah's relief, the make-up artist clearly knew her stuff. *Awesome. I must remember to ring the bride's mum next week for contact details.*

She consulted her watch. 'We have a little time before the champagne flows for the toasts. Dare I ask if this is hormones raging, or something more complicated?' This bride wouldn't be the first Zillah had known to be eating for two at her wedding breakfast.

Cara gulped and took a big, shuddery, deep breath. Zillah patted her hand, hoped the tears would hold off, and was rewarded.

'It's been just awful these last few weeks,' Cara confessed, rummaging under her skirts to produce a lace-edged silken postage stamp, presumably from her blue garter. She pressed the tiny handkerchief to her lips.

Zillah nodded. 'I can imagine. Everyone on a short fuse. No one seeming to care what you think, when it's obvious you and the groom are the only ones in the world who really matter.'

Recognition sparked in Cara's eyes. Her cheeks were no longer out-pinked by her gown. 'You understand. You really, really understand. Everyone else has been saying stuff like, 'Aunt Julia won't sit at the same table as Cousin Charles, so how do we get round that one?' Or asking me if I'm putting on weight, and frightening the daylights out of me in case my gown wouldn't fit. As it happens, I lost ten pounds, and the dressmaker was about to start force-feeding me Mars bars.'

Zillah nodded. 'Anxiety dreams?'

'Only three or four a week.'

'You poor girl. And your new husband? How's he been coping?'

'I've hardly seen Josh this last fortnight. He's been whisked off to three different stag nights. One in St Andrew's with his old university mates, one in London with his colleagues, and one in Bath with his brothers and the guys he plays squash with. Probably the man from the off-licence as well.'

Zillah nodded a second time. She wished the two of them could be chatting with a glass of something sparkly in their hands. But time wasn't on their side.

Cara was off again. 'Why does every stag night have to last three days? We've hardly had time to talk in private at all. It's as if I've married a stranger — and quite honestly, I dread the thought of two weeks alone with him. I've been longing for all the fuss to be over so we could just be together. Now it's like a big bubble's burst and I don't know what to do with myself.'

'But you still love him?'

'Of course.' Her eyes were like dinner plates. 'So, so much. I get this kind of yearning when I think of him. But sometimes lately he's been so remote, I really wonder if he still feels the same. Maybe he's gone off me and can't face confessing the truth. Maybe he'll wait till we're on honeymoon, away from our families, and blurt out that it's all a terrible mistake.' She hiccupped. 'I can't bear it.'

Zillah had to turn her head to avoid Cara seeing her smile. If only this bride knew how typical her feelings were. The whole wedding razzmatazz was on a par with life's other great rites of passage. It arrived dragging a shedload of expectations and if you were the kind of person who could tough it out, that was fine. But Cara was obviously sensitive, and right now she hurt. Playing the role of bride involved accepting a poisoned chalice in many ways. A little stealth was needed here.

'Cara, I have to go downstairs to fetch something.'

The bride pressed her fingers against her cheeks.

'Your make-up's fine, sweetheart. All you need's a touch of lip-gloss. I just need to fetch my rescue remedy drops from my bag. Be right back.'

Zillah left Cara sitting on the bed. Her heart ached for the girl. This perfect wedding-day scenario was achieved at the expense of two lost souls wondering what had possessed them to agree to put themselves through it all. As she left, she removed the sign saying *Ladies*, and pushed it back inside before gently closing the door.

Halfway down the staircase, Zillah met the bridegroom on his way up. He almost shot past her.

'Hey, just the man I was looking for!'

Josh stopped a few steps above and peered down. 'Hi, Mrs Robinson. I don't suppose you know where my fiancée — where my wife is?'

Zillah noted the anxiety in his eyes. He was probably all of twenty-five, and desperately tired of flirting with sherry-breathing great-aunts telling him how cute he used to look in a romper suit.

'Josh, the new Mrs Maxwell's in the master bedroom. I said I'd go and fetch my rescue remedy and here you are.'

He clutched the banister. 'Is she all right? I can't seem to get near her. Everyone wants a piece of us.'

'Weddings can be like that,' said Zillah. 'Cara's fine, but she's feeling a little lost. What she needs right now is a cuddle. Just tell her you love her. Tell her everything's going to be all right.'

The bridegroom took the remaining stairs two at a time.

'Josh,' called Zillah, 'I reckon your father-in-law will want to start the speeches in about ten minutes.'

'You got it!'

'Don't forget to tell Mrs Maxwell how much you love her.'

He'd vanished. She only hoped she could prise the pair of them apart once the signal came to start pouring champagne. Maybe she should have draped that veil over a chair back.

⋆　⋆　⋆

Zillah always thought the best functions were those where you cleared everything away and drew a line under the practical part, with the certainty of a cheque in the post within forty-eight hours. She and her helpers had tidied up all the catering impedimenta, leaving Jake and his friend to continue bar service and deal with the remaining glasses at the end of the evening. How satisfying for the bride's father to hand her an envelope containing a fat tip for her to share among her staff. Her crockery and cutlery were already stashed in the van, her strategy always aimed at getting in with minimum fuss and leaving in similar fashion at the end of the day.

She found her small team gathered in

the kitchen, and very pleased to receive their pay.

'You said you were going to tell me something?' Jake reminded Zillah.

'That's right. It's gone brilliantly today, guys, and I can't thank you all enough. But we shouldn't ever forget the possibility of gremlins. I once attended a wedding where a four-year-old bridesmaid released a kitten from the garden shed. The hosts had decided it would be a safe house. I'll never forget him catapulting from a window-sill. He looked like a vertical take-off craft!'

'What happened?' Abi asked.

'The kitten landed on four paws, plumb in the middle of the top tier of the wedding cake.'

She saw expressions of mixed horror and mirth upon faces.

'The bridegroom lifted the kitten off the icing and handed him to the smallest bridesmaid. The happy couple cut the cake but some guests found claw marks on their slice.'

Zillah heard laughter from behind her, and quickly turned round to see the bride standing in the kitchen doorway. She still wore her beautiful dress, minus veil, and she'd taken down her blonde hair so it hung loose down her back. Zillah marvelled at the glow you could warm your hands on. Jake and the other two young men sprang to their feet, jaws dropping.

'I didn't mean to interrupt.' Cara flashed a devastating smile at them. 'I loved your story, Mrs Robinson. It just proves nothing can spoil what's destined to be a perfect day. But I mustn't keep you. You've worked so hard, and you must be shattered. Thank you so much for all you've done.' She looked at Zillah. 'May I have a quick word before you go?'

In the impressive hallway, Cara stood on tiptoe to hug Zillah and kiss her cheek. 'I just wanted to say thanks again. For everything. Especially the rescue remedy.'

Zillah noted the sparkling eyes with

not a hint of pink. Gently taking hold of the bride's left hand, she said, 'Your wedding ring is beautiful — the perfect choice with your engagement diamond. How's that rescue remedy now?'

Cara's dimples deepened. 'In very good form. He'd been feeling the same as me. Convinced he was acting in some surreal kind of drama and wondering what it was all about. Afraid to say something in case he upset me.'

Zillah nodded. She'd read the happy couple's body language when they descended for the cake cutting. 'Soon you can forget all the trappings and get down to the reason for the whole show. You and Josh — have you been living together?'

'No. You'll probably think it's crazy, but we were both in flat-shares, and we — well, we just wanted to wait till we were married before we began a new life together.'

'I don't think it's at all crazy. I think it's lovely. And I wish you both a fountain of happiness. Just don't expect the proverbial roses all the way. Coping with the thorns is the important part.' Zillah checked her watch. 'I mustn't keep you from your wonderful party.

'And enjoy a long and happy marriage,' she added under her breath, watching the bride hitch up her train and glide away.

There was a lump like a Stonehenge standing stone clogging Zillah's throat. How come that *fountain of happiness* phrase had slipped out? Her late husband's mother had bestowed that particular wish on Zillah and Daniel at their own wedding. If only the fountain hadn't run dry so much sooner than anticipated. Now here she was, helping other couples have a happy day, while inside she was still hurting. It took her a few moments to compose herself before rejoining her team.

3

Once adrenalin-fuelled for a function, Zillah found difficulty in unwinding. On returning home, she'd unloaded dirty crocks straight from van to kitchen. It was one of the advantages of living in the garden flat. The packed lunch, eaten in a fifteen-minute break with her helpers when the family headed for church, seemed far away, and now her tummy growled for help. She wanted chicken soup, for the soul as well as for supper, probably. She enjoyed her work, but now, fixing a solitary snack on a tray, she felt an unnerving kind of restlessness. It was a bad sign.

'Hunger pangs, plus unexpected agony-aunt duty,' she muttered, taking a bottle of wine from the fridge and unscrewing the top. She'd overcome her prejudices that anything produced by a vineyard was worthless unless corked and sealed, but still went for quality rather than quantity — in her personal life as well as her business one.

Zillah stood at the sink, gazing through the window at nothing. She sometimes thought her landlady employed a magician rather than a gardener, and although their colours were dimmed by the late June evening, she knew slug-defying rows of lettuce made bright green splashes against rich dark soil. Sweet baby carrots, too tender to boil, hid beneath feathery tops. The greenhouse dripped with fragrant trusses of tomatoes. The herb garden was like a sweet-shop for Zillah, who dipped into the produce whenever she wished, repaying her landlady by freezing single portions when she held batch casserole-making sessions.

She sipped her wine, looking forward to her soup and rustic loaf supper. Suddenly, she realised she had no recollection of feeding the cats. On days when she fed crowds, she sometimes felt as if she should give a sermon to accompany the loaves and fishes. Her landlady was away . . . ah, yes — now of course she remembered opening cans for Velma, Roxy and Ruby.

As if on cue, Velma, jet-black with one pure white ear, appeared from behind the runner beans and sashayed down the path towards the house. She headed for the catflap in the utility room door, flashing a look at Zillah as if to say, *What are you staring at?*

Zillah carried her supper into the sitting-room and switched on the television without much hope. Maybe she should select a DVD, but somehow she couldn't be bothered. A couple circled a dance floor. The man gave the impression of longing to look down at what his feet were doing, rather like a learner driver changing gear. He wore a slashed gold sequinned top. This was a programme not, strictly speaking, to Zillah's taste, but it would provide something to glance at while she ate.

'Some mindless telly will relax me,' she told herself.

She thought the man wearing the sequinned top looked familiar, and might have been a moonlighting weather presenter. She suddenly thought of Hal Christmas and chuckled, imagining those broad shoulders squeezed into a sequinned waistcoat. Macho men in sparkles made for a provocative image; and, it occurred to her, this was the first time she'd thought of this infuriating chunk of eye-candy since her morning chat with Abi. Relaxed she was not.

* * *

In a ramshackle cottage, only a few miles away from Zillah, Hal had abandoned his unpacking, and was once more wondering what miserable fate would have propelled such a devastating-looking, yet acid-tongued, blonde into his orbit. How could someone with eyes rivalling the colour of violets be so uptight? What was the witch's problem? After their near-collision, when they sat exchanging insults, his hand had hovered over the gear stick, ready to engage fast reverse. That was before it occurred to him that the beautiful but bad-tempered diva might actually prove useful.

She'd sent him in the right direction, and his inspection had convinced him to rent the unit. He hadn't got off on the right foot as regarded being good neighbours; but far worse than a male-versus-female driver incident was the worrying fact that both of them traded under almost the same name.

To complicate matters, Hal knew he was the one who must back down. This wasn't an action he was used to pulling off. He'd capitulated in spectacular fashion as a young, inexperienced accountant, consequently missing out on an important promotion. He'd vowed never again to allow anyone to intimidate him — even a woman with curves he couldn't get out of his mind, and in whose hair he longed to bury his face.

Hal reached for his phone, searched for the *Mrs Robinson* number, and left a voicemail message, asking her if they could possibly meet on Monday.

★ ★ ★

Next morning, Zillah served the divas their tuna delicacy in the utility room. The feline trio were up to High Doh, the smallest one shooting across the floor and rubbing herself against Zillah's ankle, chattering like a motor engine.

'Don't let those big girls eat your share, Ruby,' Zillah whispered to the little cat, in two minds whether to scoop her up and spoil her. There was a leftover half chicken breast in the fridge, but it would only cause trouble. The other two would probably gang up on Ruby, even hiss tales to her landlady when Clarissa returned from her travels. Zillah smiled at her nonsensical thinking, hardened her heart, and left them to it.

The whole day stretched ahead. She should take herself off for a walk. Walking alone was a chance to clear her thoughts. When she returned, she'd put her timetable for the week on the laptop and email it from her personal address to her business one. Next Saturday she was catering a wedding reception for a hundred and fifty. This was taking place in a marquee in the grounds of a stunning Regency house, and preparations were well in hand.

Later, she'd go into work and make more petits fours so they could dry, be painted with egg white, and rest ready for packing in waxed paper. The wedding cake, three dark and delicious tiers already baked, was currently in the hands of an artisan who decorated Zillah's celebration cakes, transforming them into wondrous creations. The tiers of this cake would be cloudlike, the icing dusted with gold leaf to match the bridal gown. Sadly, their expertise didn't come cheap, therefore leaving very little profit for *Mrs Robinson*.

* * *

At noon, Zillah arrived at Planet Robinson, as Abi called their workplace. The first thing she noticed was the black Jeep next to her usual space. Did this man have no home to go to? As it was Sunday, she parked parallel to the building. Childish it might be, but she found the thought of their two vehicles side by side oddly off-putting.

She hesitated beside her van. Then, deciding to unload the clean crockery later, she let herself into her office where she found the answerphone light flashing. She listened to the only message, grimacing as the caller announced himself. She could meet him tomorrow, but her response could wait until first thing next morning.

Meticulous about hygiene whatever day of the week it was, she pulled on her work clogs, apron and hat before unlocking the food preparation area. The kitchen, left immaculate after disgorging yesterday's feast, gleamed as if telling her to get going and make it look as if it had a life. She filled the kettle, then reached for her stainless-steel basin and the big pan she used when melting chocolate. From the dry goods store-cupboard she took two packs of cocoa-rich confectioner's couverture. These she unwrapped and placed in a plastic bag which she tapped with a rolling pin, preparing the blocks for melting and forming the glossy basis of a nut-and-dried-fruit concoction. Drizzling orange liqueur over the chunks, she filled the pan from the steaming kettle, leaving the basin perched above the simmering water.

Zillah took down her favourite copper weighing scales from the shelf above, ignoring the state-of-the-art digital version Abi preferred. She placed a weight on the stand and tipped almonds, walnuts and golden sultanas into the oval bowl. Next, she switched on the extraction unit. Open windows were great, but sugary smells invited winged invaders, and the UK summer scored high on the 'vacations for wasps' website.

There was no sound of anyone else being in the building. When she glanced outside, she saw hers was the only vehicle on the forecourt. Good. He must have left without her noticing. She'd no desire to fritter away time with Mr Christmas before their appointed meeting, but she wondered what exactly he planned on doing up there. Did he not need just a telephone, computer and filing cabinet? These items would fit into even an average-size bedsit room. Did he really intend to audition acts in his office? She'd spoken in jest, but now wondered if it might be true.

Zillah peered into the rich well of melting chocolate. It smelt divine. It shone like satin. But she wouldn't disturb it until she was sure of its perfection. Only then would she probe with the fine skewer designed for testing sponge cakes. She reached for a pack of miniature foil cups and arranged them on a baking sheet, ready for moving to the walk-in pantry.

Job finished, she could almost smell that cup of coffee. Carefully, she carried the tray and shut it away, came back and ran water into the scraped-clean bowl. Her hand was reaching for the first-size cafetière when she heard a tap on the door.

Why did her heart flip when it should have sunk? Had Mr Christmas returned without her hearing his engine? There was no way to pretend she wasn't there. A tall person could easily peer through the clear-glazed window panel. And he was certainly tall. She opened the door.

'Good morning. I brought a peace offering.' His gaze travelled lazily over her, his eyes amused.

Zillah tensed. *Okay, Mr Christmas. My outfit might not raise pulse rates, but it proves I'm looking after my livelihood.*

He, on the other hand, looked annoyingly relaxed in a pale-grey long-sleeved T-shirt and black jeans not tight enough to make him appear to be trying too hard. There was a Sunday paper tucked under his left arm. Propped against his chest was a cardboard box displaying the logo of her favourite supermarket. He was, she thought, temptation on legs.

'I thought it might be sensible if we shared a cup of coffee and got to know one another a bit.' He raised an eyebrow.

'I only just picked up your phone message.'

'But this is Sunday. I imagine you do allow yourself the occasional break?'

She knew it would be churlish to refuse. 'My office is unlocked,' she said. 'Take a seat and read your paper. I was about to make a brew.'

She reached for the second-size cafetière. What, she wondered, had brought about this sudden thaw?

When Zillah entered her office again,

she almost drooled. The open cake box contained two squares of honey-soaked baklava. Beside these sat two fresh fruit tartlets, juicy red berries nestling in confectioner's custard swirled with cream. Her unwanted guest, one long leg slung over the other, was browsing the sports section of the newspaper. She averted her gaze from his feet, big and bare in buttery leather loafers.

He looked up and smiled at her. Today his eyes were barley-sugar. Like kitten Ruby's were.

'Can I do anything?'

'Just tell me if you take milk or sugar.'

'Neither, thanks.' He rose and looked down at her. This immensely pleasurable experience caused her to focus elsewhere and fast. She remembered what Abi had said about his height. An instant desire to hide within the shelter of his arms hit her, dismaying her with its intensity.

'Would you like to point me in the direction of the plates and knives?' He followed her as far as the kitchen doorway.

She felt disarmed by his concern not to breach her rules, almost as if she was the one in the wrong.

'The coffee needs a couple more minutes.' She handed him plates, paper serviettes and knives.

He retreated. Zillah tore off her hat, smoothed down her hair and unfastened her apron, jigging up and down with impatience when her fingers didn't free the knotted strings fast enough. She pulled up her T-shirt and sniffed under both arms. All was well. She shucked off her bovver boots and divided the contents of the cafetière between two thin porcelain mugs. Barefoot, carrying the drinks carefully, she walked through to join her visitor.

He rose and went round to her side of the desk, pulling out the chair. 'Coffee smells great. But then you're a professional,' he said. 'No milk for you either?'

'Nor sugar.'

His huge laugh rumbled. It was the first time she'd heard him let rip his voice. If dark brown velvet could be made audible, this had to be how it would sound. He was close enough to reward her with a hint of cologne. Her mouth dried and, to her fury, her stomach lurched again.

'What's so funny?' She so needed to ground herself on Planet Robinson.

'You and me. Black coffee addicts about to get high on sticky pastries.' He put a plate before her and held the box so she could choose first. 'Come on. No one's watching.'

She couldn't take her eyes off his mouth. He'd better be a tidy eater. If just one crumb should linger on that top lip, she doubted her ability not to lick her fingertip and lean closer.

Robbed of her power to concentrate, she felt relieved when Hal Christmas quizzed her on good places to eat in and around Bath. By tacit agreement, they totally avoided the enormous animal with a trunk sitting in the corner

— until he insisted on showing off his handiwork on the top floor.

'Come upstairs with me a moment,' he said, rising.

She followed him, trying to keep her imagination under control and painfully aware of her legs turning to jelly with every step. 'It certainly seems more welcoming now,' she said, relieved to focus upon the creamy walls and buttercup-gloss window-frames resulting from his DIY skills.

'I'm so used to number-crunching, I'd forgotten how much I enjoy working with my hands.'

She was forced to tiptoe across the dust-sheeted floor to the window and take a deep breath before her thoughts raced off with her serenity. Serenity? Who was she kidding? She was no better than that naughty little puss, Velma.

'I'm having blinds fitted in the morning. Carpet tiles in the afternoon.' He hesitated. 'Ach! You must be bored to screaming point. I'm sorry, Zillah. I may call you Zillah?'

She could do nothing else but nod.

'I know we'll be laying our cards on the table tomorrow. You can make tomorrow, I hope?'

She nodded. Again.

'Excellent. But I think I need to say, if I've caused you any inconvenience whatsoever, then I apologise. I was out of order. I hit upon the name two years ago when I was a partner in a London accountancy firm.'

'Two years ago. But — ' Zillah couldn't believe this.

He held out his hands, palms upwards. 'Please let me explain. At that time, to my knowledge there was no business trading as *Mrs Robinson*. And remember, I was still living in London. I acquired one or two actors among my accountancy clients.' He walked over to the window and stood beside her. 'You may or may not be surprised to learn to what lengths luvvies will go when they're resting and the rent's due. I enjoyed their anecdotes. I discovered a whole new culture.'

Zillah raised her eyebrows. She hadn't expected his life story. Hopefully it would stop her fantasising about him nuzzling her neck.

'One day, my neighbour told me she wanted to hire a children's entertainer. I researched and booked one. Her yummy mummy mates latched on. I liked the idea of a bit of light relief from my day job, and there it was.' His face darkened. 'When my personal circumstances changed, I decided to relocate.' He paused and turned to face her. 'I relish a challenge.'

Suddenly she longed to find out what had triggered his need to relocate. Longed to know if he lived anywhere near her, and whether or not he was on his own, though that seemed unlikely. How could someone who seemed so unapproachable make her feel the way she did? *It's too soon.*

Her schedule nagged her. She checked her watch and broke the spell.

'Enough already. The rest can wait

until we meet tomorrow.' He pushed his hand through his hair. 'I have a load of stuff to sort out.'

Back downstairs, tidying her workplace and collecting linen for laundering, Zillah decided it best to wait until early next day to start another batch of petits fours.

She set the alarm, double-locked the outer door, and was almost at the van when she remembered the crockery. Well, it would just have to stay where it was until tomorrow. This out-of-character attitude startled her. This whole weekend seemed slightly surreal. Zillah liked routine. It kept her going. Already she was anticipating her usual Sunday evening with a good book, glass of wine and plate of nibbles, followed by an early bedtime.

★ ★ ★

Hal was back to the chaos of the over-stuffed thatched cottage that was his new home. He sighed as he unlocked the front door and gave it the customary shove with his shoulder in order to gain access. He must do something about that. Damp had a lot to answer for. In the hallway he had to side-step boxes and bulging black plastic bags. Using the back door would only be an option if he wielded the strimmer that had never figured on his shopping list in his London flat-dwelling days. He'd never imagined himself moving to the country. Jessie had adored city living.

But, though they had lived together for almost three years, he'd always felt she was marking time with him. His pride was hurt when she moved out, leaving him with an emptiness he found depressing. He consoled himself by planning a drastic change in his lifestyle after Jessie proved him right by taking a job in Amsterdam. Hurt pride he could cope with. It would fade. A sense of time slipping away and nobody to share his leisure hours with presented more of a problem.

His flat would sell at a profit. Eventually. Money-wise, he had eggs in several baskets, and the world — or, rather, the UK — was open to him. He deliberately chose not to live in a city. But he wasn't daft enough to consider donning green wellies and buying a smallholding halfway up a mountain. One of his clients had owned a second home near Bath. It was in an attractive place called Bradford-on-Avon, and Hal had visited and taken a liking to the countryside.

He had thrown ideas in the air and waited to see how they landed. Taking a gamble, he handed in his notice, having talked things through with his close colleagues. Their suggestion that he should be retained as a consultant boosted his ego — and, potentially, his finances. His fellow partners probably reckoned they'd wave goodbye to more than one valued client if they didn't do a little carrot-dangling. He was, after all, planning to become another bead threaded on the long necklace that was the M4 motorway.

He went upstairs, stripped to his boxers and pulled on a pair of faded khaki shorts and a T-shirt saying *Something for the Weekend*. His computer and various books and files made up part of the downstairs clutter. Office equipment was to be delivered mid-week, but he was fired up to create some space. He wouldn't leave it until morning in case it rained again. His colleagues had teased him about moving not to the West, but to the West Country, yet he still felt he'd made the right decision.

He clattered back downstairs, propped open the sulky front door, and went out to the car. The boot still held all the kit he'd used to paint his new office. He groaned. He owned a garage, but it was packed with junk like an antiquated lawnmower and boxes containing colonies of empty jam jars. He'd need to ask around. There was sure to be someone local who would take them off his hands.

Or were women too high-powered to make jam these days? Spiders scuttled as he double-stacked boxes to make space for his decorating equipment.

He wondered how the lovely Mrs Robinson would spend the rest of her day. She hadn't mentioned a Mr Robinson — or anything else relating to a personal life. It was no business of his. He just hoped they could work something out regarding the name clash. Maybe he should ring his lawyer buddy and establish his position. What a pain. What a way to start a new business. What a good job he enjoyed trouble-shooting. And what a good job he'd decided living with one ambitious career woman was more than enough. Zillah might be a stunning woman, but if there was a man in her life, he must need the protection of a safety helmet and flak jacket.

But Hal wanted her. He wanted her so much that just picturing the shape of her pretty mouth jolted him in the solar plexus.

4

By nine next morning, rows of Zillah's plump and rosy marzipan fruits were lined up on wire trays. Next up was a batch of crunchy brown-sugar meringue Pavlova bases. She could do without meeting Hal Christmas later; but, although certain of her rights, she didn't intend to give an inch and risk letting him trample over them. Hopefully he'd back down and tell her he planned to choose a new trading name.

The telephone rang. She picked up on the extension.

'*Mrs Robinson.*'

'Good morning. I wonder if Hal's around. Are you his secretary?'

She sucked in her breath, tempted to pretend and hear more of these dark chocolate tones. 'Might I enquire if this is a catering enquiry?'

'Sorry? I'm trying to make contact with Hal Christmas but he seems to have got a new mobile number. I remembered him emailing something about starting a new business called *Mrs Robinson*, so I typed it into a search engine and found you.'

'Well, if you'd paid more attention, you'd have noticed *my* company offers a gourmet catering service. Mr Christmas and his capering clowns have no connection with us whatsoever.'

Silence. The caller seemed to digest this. 'What a crock,' he said at last.

'I couldn't agree more.' Zillah relented. This man sounded much more human than Hal. 'Mr Christmas has leased the office above mine. I can relay a message if you like.' *If I must.*

'You can? That's really very kind. Ask him to give me a call, would you? Zak Silver's the name. He'll know. I'm very sorry to have troubled you. I must have got the wrong end of the stick.'

'I can assure you, this isn't your fault. I'll make sure your friend gets your message.' She rang off.

Now, wasn't that the perfect name for an entertainer? It had to be made up. Briefly, she wondered what particular talent Mr Silver focused upon in order to make a living. Surely he wasn't a clown or a conjuror? That sexy voice must surely belong to a singer. She put such thoughts behind her, tuned in her radio to the afternoon drama, and set about whisking egg whites into clouds. She wanted those bases in the big oven so they'd dry out before she finished for the day.

To her delight, *The African Queen* was just about to sail up the river. Zillah was immersed in the play, enjoying the banter between Rose and Charlie, when she realised something was happening outside. She could hear voices and she'd been vaguely aware of vehicles arriving but that was what happened weekdays. She peeped out anyway. A van belonging to a local firm was parked nearby. Of course, the upstairs office blinds were being fitted.

'Oh, bananas,' she muttered. She couldn't pass on that phone message from Zak Silver without physically leaving her office and poking her nose into his domain. Guiltily, she remembered the gold business card sitting on her coffee table at home. Well, she was a busy person and couldn't be expected to take note of every single thing. No doubt Abi had committed the number to memory, but she wasn't in today. Zillah wasn't prepared to act as Mr Christmas's answering service. The sooner he got himself both a landline and name change, the better.

Slipping through to her office, she wrote RING ZAK SILVER on a Post-it Note, went to the outer door and gazed around. The man fitting the blinds was obviously upstairs. The door to the stairs gaped and loud pop music filtered from on high, drowning her call of 'Hello!'. She tried to stick the fluorescent pink rectangle to the banister, but the note fell off and plummeted to the floor.

Zillah closed her eyes and counted to ten. On five, she heard the stairs creak and opened her eyes again, only to see a pair of leather loafers, followed by long legs in navy blue trousers, making their way downwards. A white shirt was tucked into the trousers. The trim midriff suffered neither from beer belly nor thickening waistline. The feet halted. For the second time in a matter of days, she found herself craning her neck to gaze at an attractive man.

Saturday's young bridegroom on the Nancarrow staircase had proved easy to handle. All Zillah's senses yelled at her not to get close to Hal Christmas. If she didn't stop ogling him in just one split second, he would begin to think she had designs on him.

'Well, here's to you, Mrs Robinson. Though I doubt they'll be playing your song on that radio station the blinds-fitters favour.' He grinned as if no one else in the world had pulled that one on her before, and jerked his head, indicating the cacophony from upstairs.

'Mr Christmas,' she said icily. 'Good morning. I've already taken one call meant for you.' She held out the fluorescent pink Post-it Note. 'If I pick up any more enquiries not intended for the real *Mrs Robinson*, I suggest it's best I relay them at our meeting this afternoon.'

He was standing beside her now. Towering over her. A drift of the kind of cologne men's grandmas don't buy them hit her. Different from the hand-blended one Daniel had used — different, but equally unsettling. Just as she'd finally come to terms with her single state, this hulking great male who possessed the ability to tap into her baser instincts had arrived on the scene. It really wasn't fair, especially as the only occasions he'd seen her — apart from in her van — coincided with her wearing a prim apron, Puritan head-scarf and silly boots. If she was very lucky, maybe he'd offer her some pantomime dame gigs later in the year.

'Zillah — I mean, Mrs Robinson

— no, this is silly. I'm sorry about this, Zillah. I promise to explain everything later.' Hal took the Post-it Note from her, his fingers warm against hers.

Zillah, who had sorely missed the touch of a hand, the comfort of friendly contact — especially when it was human and male — jumped as if stung. Fortunately, he didn't notice. His attention focused on her handwritten message.

'Good lord,' he said. 'That reprobate rang? Last I heard of Zak Silver, he was working in Las Vegas.'

'Fascinating.' Zillah's tone would have rendered cryonic technology obsolete. 'He seemed quite keen to speak to you. Such a pity you didn't circulate your address book with your new contact details.'

Hal Christmas was gazing at her. Or was it a glare? Either way, she found it difficult to outstare him.

'Your place or mine? For our meeting, I mean,' He looked enquiringly at her.

What else would he have meant?

'Do you have enough chairs for two people?' She hoped her gaze challenged him. But the disturbing way his eyes changed colour distracted her. Now they were darkest butterscotch, reminiscent of snooty diva Velma's.

'Affirmative,' he said. 'Unless you object to a folding seat. I also possess a kettle and mugs. Don't forget to leave your answerphone on.'

Zillah held up one hand. 'Fair enough. You want to christen your office. I'll be there at four.'

'Can't wait, Mrs. Robinson.'

She turned away. She was determined to keep their dealings strictly businesslike, but his self-importance riled her. Whatever she did, she mustn't take it out on her meringues.

★ ★ ★

One of Zillah's elderly ladies who lunched rang to order chicken casserole and strawberry trifle for six. This was

66

how *Mrs Robinson* had begun. Sandwich orders for sales conferences led to requests for upmarket food for board meetings. Zillah's initial leaflet drop included hairdressers, beauty salons and boutiques, all places where women went. This week, she was due to deliver a buffet lunch for thirty members of a women's group to the home of their chairman, continue preparation for the weekend wedding feast, and slot in the equally important luncheon for six ladies.

'You have to stay positive,' she told herself when she sat down at her computer around one o'clock. 'All businesses take a while to get going.'

Like Jake had said when she'd had coffee in the pub, lots of people began planning Christmas parties once the calendar page flipped over to September. Oh, why did that annoying man come equipped with such a surname?

Briefly, she wondered what it must be like to go through life as Mrs Christmas. Wouldn't everyone just love it when they called your name at the dental surgery? Did his wife plan on having any little helpers one day after she got bored with high-flying? Surely a man like him would be partnered with Superwoman. Anyway, why wasn't she taking time out to help her man organize his new premises? Unless, as main breadwinner, the lady just couldn't be spared. Maybe that was why he was so surly at times. His wife probably wore the trousers.

Zillah convinced herself such a couple must be truly sorted. Mrs Christmas would return to her luxury loft on weeknights, convenient for her job smashing glass ceilings in the City, while her husband chilled out in their chic cottage, playing with his new business venture. No doubt he presented his missus with a bowl of homemade soup and a crusty artisan loaf when she returned to their rural love nest, frazzled from her Friday night motorway journey.

Zillah was on the point of deciding

whether Mrs Christmas was a Jemima or a Sophie when she told herself to pull herself together. There was a request to quote for a Bar Mitzvah party in Zillah's inbox. She fired off a response, then sent emails to firms she already dealt with, plus some she didn't. Just before four, she picked up a plastic folder and slid some of her publicity material inside, adding glossy photographs of luscious foods. She included a showpiece of an enormous joint of roast pork, its impressive criss-cross crackling gleaming crunchy dark gold. Her most powerful weapon, she gloated, was a document giving her company's date of registration, directors and registered address.

Hesitating, she wondered whether she should take something edible with her but decided against it, in case he might consider the gesture cosy. Though she'd pitch her homemade shortbread and Abi's meringues against the baked goods he'd bought, yummy though they had been.

She heard a phone ring just as she reached the top of the stairs. The door to the front office stood open, revealing Hal standing by the window, mobile pressed to an ear. He waved to Zillah, mouthing 'Sit down'.

She chose the nearest chair, moving it further away from its companion before placing her folder on the empty green-baize card table.

'Zak,' said Hal. 'Of course I'm pleased to speak to you, man. Thanks for ringing back, but I'm just about to go into a meeting — no, of course I'm not trying to make excuses.' Hal stopped speaking, then said, 'I'll ring you later. Speak soon.'

Zillah, aware of his gaze, avoided making eye contact. She glanced at her watch and swung one black-trousered leg over the other. She inspected the toe of her burnished burgundy leather pump against the bare floor, and wondered what shade he'd chosen for his new carpet tiles.

He walked towards her and put down

his phone. 'Coffee?'

'No thanks. I'd prefer to get on. Busy week.'

'Of course.' He took the other seat. 'What do you think of the blinds?'

'They do what they're meant to do. As a matter of interest, why do you need to bump up your outgoings on office premises when presumably you could work from home?'

He shuffled in his seat, grimacing as if finding it difficult to get comfortable. 'Furniture arrives later this week,' he said. 'In answer to your question, I also intend on running my accountancy practice from these premises. Why? I don't fancy being overrun with files and reference books in my bijou residence down the valley. Plus I happen to live at the bottom of a vicious track bent on devouring unsuspecting vehicles. My cottage boasts an entrance I drove past three times on the day I arrived to view it. By comparison, finding this retail estate is like standing on the Thames Embankment and locating the river.'

She opened her mouth to speak, but he wasn't finished.

'Nor is it, I imagine, a total suspension of disbelief to imagine that the occasional entertainer will call by to introduce himself, or indeed herself or themselves. When I'm wearing my party hat, so to speak, if anyone insists on demonstrating their fire-eating skills, I promise to warn you first so you can have your conflagration blanket at the ready.'

Of course he was trying to wind her up. But his eyes were no longer the disdainful amber of earlier: rather, a mellow toffee shade, glinting with merriment. He'd put on a snazzy dark-blue tie with green jellyfish float-ing across it. Was this for her benefit? He was unlike any accountant she'd ever come across in her faraway office days. Her left hand reached for the plump, polished ebony heart she wore swinging from a fine gold chain round her neck. The honeymoon gift from Daniel acted as her talisman.

'I was hoping we could become friends, Zillah.' Hal spoke softly. 'At the very least, not enemies.'

Don't give in to him. 'So why did you burst onto my patch without a by your leave?'

He looked hurt. 'I've already apologised for stealing your name. What more can I do? I fully intend on sorting this out. It's just that I haven't got round to choosing another title for the entertainment agency yet. Give me a couple more days, and hopefully you may find having our two businesses coexisting beneath one roof provides a lucrative spin off.'

Zillah was nonplussed. He'd played to her emotions yesterday, trying to soften her up. Today, she'd anticipated having to argue her case. Defend her rights. And possibly consult her solicitor. Something, she thought guiltily, she should have done already, but just hadn't got around to. Not only did she feel relieved, she could hear Abi's voice saying *I told you so.*

'The publicity you've already under-taken?' She mustn't take her eye off the ball. 'I imagine there are flyers as well as business cards doing the rounds.'

He rose, affecting an exaggerated limp. 'Ouch! You wouldn't want to linger too long on those chairs.' He walked over to the window and stretched his arms above his head. 'As for PR, it's just business cards at the moment. They won't break the bank. I must have thrown them at most of the bigger Bath hotels, and if people ring my mobile then there's no problem.'

She nodded.

'As soon as the landline's connected and I have my new trading name, I'll be asking you to recommend a local printer, and probably someone to build a website. I do understand the impor-tance of that.'

Again came that crinkly-eyed grin with its devastating effect on her stomach. *Damn him.*

'All right,' said Zillah. 'I must admit, I'm relieved to find you so amenable.'

He made no response. She inspected her neatly-manicured nails. When she glanced up again, he was gazing at the locket nestling just above her cleavage. She felt her cheeks warming. This man spelled danger even when he didn't switch on the charm. Again, she wished she hadn't decided to meet him on his territory. On the defensive, she felt she was trying to prove her business integrity to him, rather than the reverse.

'I have to say, I'm rather hurt that you appear to have such a negative impression of me.'

'You can hardly blame me for that.'

'Hmm,' mused Hal. 'I can imagine it must have been a surprise to have your phone ring, then answer it to find someone demanding a DJ.'

'It was the request for a troop of hot singing waiters that floored me.'

For moments, they gazed at each other. Zillah broke the silence first. Hal seemed startled but burst out laughing too.

'Oh, God, I'm so sorry.' He held his

hands out, palms upended.

'Don't worry about it. You've made a big hit with my assistant.' Zillah refrained from adding the ageist comment.

'Abi enjoys the luxury of working for a good employer with none of the pressures of keeping the show on the road. So, dare I ask how much input in the business Mr Robinson has?'

Zillah folded her arms. 'Not a lot. I was widowed twenty months ago.'

5

After Zillah left, the only available surface against which Hal felt he could justifiably bang his head was the wall. But, given he'd so recently rolled two coats of country buttercup emulsion over it, he felt disinclined to deface the perfection of his paintwork.

He wondered why Abi hadn't marked his card to prevent him from making the kind of faux pas he just had. But, to be fair, why should she have? It was hardly his business. He'd merely been making conversation, trying to detain the lovely enigma that was Zillah, if he was honest.

He'd planned to ask her advice over renaming his agency. 'Hal Christmas' was how his accountancy clients knew him, and he didn't intend changing that. But this sideline, that he believed expressed a side of the Hal left buried for too long — didn't it deserve an appropriate name? Zillah was a creative person. It would be fun to share an ideas-fest with her. If he had one weakness where women were concerned, it centred on cool blondes, despite having fallen for slinky brunette Jessie in what seemed a different lifetime.

It was a pity about Mrs Robinson — in more ways than one. Zillah hadn't seemed keen to hang around after his tactless query crashed and burned. Who could blame her? She must have guts, though. She could only have been on her own for about six months before starting her catering business. Hal wondered what she'd been doing before. Did she have children? If so, they could be teenagers. She was probably in her early to mid-thirties. Her slim, athletic figure suggested healthy eating and working out.

He smiled, picturing her tucking into those gooey cakes. Had that really been only yesterday? He didn't like women who got precious about food. It was all about balance. Zillah was living proof of his theory. She'd look great in a jogging suit. She'd look great in anything. Or nothing . . .

All of this was academic. Mrs Robinson was wedded to her catering enterprise. And who could blame her? He hadn't a clue as to how long the recovery period lasted after bereavement. Did she have children? The teenage offspring to whom she might well now be a single parent would doubtless be very protective of their mum. Zillah was, unsurprisingly, defensive. A lone woman, running a business, must be able to cover her back. To his surprise, he found himself worrying about her personal security. He told himself to stop being so stupid and to get on with some work.

Through the open window, Hal heard voices drifting from below. Approaching with caution, he peered out and bit his lip. Zillah, hands on hips, was informing the carpet tile fitter her door definitely didn't access any other premises, and if it did, she'd surely have noticed. Another nail in the coffin. Though, in the circumstances, that too was a gaffe.

★ ★ ★

'So how did the meeting go?' Abi paused before getting into her work gear next morning.

'Good, thanks.'

'Did he surrender?'

'In a word, yes.'

'Thought so.' Zillah detected a hint of triumph. 'So you're friends?'

'Erm, I sort of blew it.'

'Go on.' Abi was reaching for her whites. She put her head round the door. 'Don't tell me Hal asked you on a date and you turned him down.'

'Of course not. He asked about Mr Robinson's input.'

'Ah.' Abi walked across the kitchen and pulled up a stool beside Zillah. 'I'm so sorry. I should have said something to him. I mean, you can hardly criticise the guy for being interested. You're gorgeous, and — '

'About the right age for an old man?' Zillah teased.

Abi blushed. 'Absolutely not. You know what? My boyfriend's convinced you must've been a model. And you can't have missed the way Mickey straightens his tie the minute you walk through his door.' She stood up and put her arms round Zillah. 'You cope so brilliantly. I can only imagine how much you miss your husband. He must've been an absolute sweetie if he was married to you.'

Zillah hugged her back. 'Thank you, Abi. Yes, Daniel was an absolute sweetie.'

'Hal must be beating himself up over it,' said Abi.

'Do you think? I can't imagine that man allowing himself the luxury of emotions.' Zillah peered through the window to see a dark-green van pulling up. She recognised the florist. Their paths often crossed, and each held a stock of the other's business cards.

Mel, proprietor of the business, hopped out and opened her van's back doors. Holding a lavish bouquet almost her height, she spotted Zillah and waved at her to come to the door.

'Mustn't stop.' Mel handed over a cellophane-wrapped deluge of carnations, freesias and feathery foliage. 'I hope these are from some gorgeous guy. My assistant dealt with the telephone order, so I didn't speak to whoever it was. Let's have lunch one day so I can interrogate you. I owe you one for recommending me to that boutique hotel in the Crescent.'

Zillah stood, arms full, watching Mel jump back into the driver's seat. The van reared on its back wheels and roared off. It was just as well that king-of-the-road Hal Christmas was otherwise engaged, and couldn't encounter the flying florist headlamp-to-headlamp.

'Here you are, boss.' Abi crossed the

room, holding Zillah's mug. 'Coffee dark as sin. Wow! It's not your birthday is it?'

'*Mrs Robinson*'s birthday is this week. Mine was in May. Don't fret. You did send me a card.' Zillah's fingers found a miniature white envelope. She put it down and propped the bouquet in one of the sinks.

Abi passed the scissors. She refrained from further comment, her expression showing how difficult she found this.

'I told you I had a good feel about the Nancarrow wedding.' Zillah slit open the envelope. 'I didn't expect flowers, though. You should share these with your — ' Her words faded at the sight of the message card. Her brow creased.

The telephone rang.

'I'll take it in your office,' said Abi.

Zillah felt reluctant to reveal the sender's identity. She wished he hadn't done this. It wasn't necessary, and it was the last thing she needed. Hal Christmas wasn't helping matters, even though the gesture was doubtless well-meant. She couldn't pass the bouquet off as a gift from grateful clients after offering half the freesias to Abi. Well, she could, but her assistant, although a darling, was also a chatter-box and if she bumped into Hal, which she surely would, given she was such a fan, she might easily tell him how well Saturday's wedding went and what fabulous flowers the bride's parents had sent Zillah as a token of their appreciation.

She tucked the card into her trouser pocket. The seven-word message was written in Mel's curly script: *I apologise for treading on your dreams. HC.*

Zillah could imagine the florist speculating as she wrote it. But she understood the message's significance, and that unnerved her. It proved the sender was in tune with her passion for making her business succeed, as well as with her bereavement. Most significant of all, Zillah's book of poetry flopped open every time at the Yeats poem, she'd read it so often.

Abi bounded back. '*Electron* want us to provide a boardroom lunch on the twentieth — rustic sandwiches for twelve people. The CEO's PA is on maternity leave so the temp rang. I've left the message on your desk. She sounded in a bit of a flap, so I told her we know the fillings they like and you'll email confirmation as usual.'

'Well done, Abi. Poor lady, I wonder how long she'll last. I'm told that particular gentleman can sniff out fear at twenty paces.' Zillah glanced again at the flowers. 'I must put these in water. They're nothing to do with the Nancarrow wedding. I must have mentioned the firm's first birthday when I met with Hal Christmas — maybe I shouldn't be so hard on him. This is a very thoughtful gesture.'

A tall figure strode past the window, heading for his car. Zillah glanced up automatically. She felt her stomach lurch, looked away, and hurriedly cleared her throat.

She noticed Abi studying her, a very smug expression on her face.

'What?' Zillah stood, hands on hips.

'Nothing. I'll make a start on the sponge bases, shall I?'

★ ★ ★

She'd ploughed her fingers through it so often, Zillah's hair resembled a spiky coronet. Her original business plan had proved good enough to convince the bank to agree to a modest loan, and her record-keeping was efficient. But she still needed to analyse her trading figures because something wasn't right. Probably she'd got one of those Da Vinci Code things in a twist; because no matter how hard she tried to get her head round formulae, she struggled, in spite of the spreadsheet course she'd taken to help gain jobs in the past. At the moment she was reluctant to pay accountancy fees.

'Maybe I should give up wine. Stop buying books and DVDs.' Spoken aloud, it sounded a gloomy proposition. It wasn't as if her leisure hours sparkled. It was fortunate she enjoyed walking through the city's parks as well as exploring its beating heart. She enjoyed watching squirrels scamper around their woodland playground. She also loved café society, adored checking out restaurant menus and people-watching. Other folk's parties were her social life.

She jumped at the sound of someone banging on the outer door, locked as soon as Abi left at five o'clock. Cautiously, she got up to take a peek. Through the reinforced glass pane she saw the back of a tall man wearing black leather jacket, jeans and desert boots. He was staring at the vehicles still in the car park. Hmm. She was a lone female. It was nearly six p.m. She was entitled to be at home with her feet up by now, and certainly to ignore an out-of-hours visitor. But you never knew. This might mean a new contact, and if you were in business you didn't reject opportunities. She made a decision. Abi kept nagging her about getting a safety-chain fixed, and Zillah resolved to see to it the following day.

She opened the front door. The caller spun round to face her. He was older now she stood face to face with him, late thirties rather than twenties. He wore his glossy brown hair in a shaggy, attractive style, and his suntan had to be natural. He wasn't movie-star handsome, but his cheeky grin was designed to melt even the grimmest of people.

'Hi there. I'm here to see Hal Christmas.' He raised his voice on the last syllable.

Zillah glanced at the nearly empty car park. 'Doesn't seem to be here, I'm afraid.'

'Not a problem. I'm early. Do you have a reception area?'

She smoothed her hair. 'Mr Christmas's offices are totally separate from mine.'

The man waved at her signboard.

'I'm still confused. Are there two firms with the same name?'

'Not any more. What time's your appointment?'

'Six o'clock. Hey, I can wait in my car. I'm sure Hal will ring me if he's been delayed.'

Zillah thought quickly. She had her street cred to consider. If people started telling Hal Christmas she was unfriendly, he might question whether to send business her way. It was a no-brainer.

'You can wait in my office if you like. I'll open the window so we can listen for his car.'

The visitor grinned and held out his hand. 'Zak Silver's the name. You answered the phone to me, didn't you? I recognise that lovely voice. So, whom do I have the pleasure of addressing?'

She shook his hand. 'Zillah Robinson. And before you ask, yes, it's Mrs Robinson. Come this way.'

Zak waited till Zillah was seated behind her desk. Then he turned his chair round and sat astride it, arms folded on its back. A low whistle left his lips. 'Wow, that's a beautiful desk.'

'Thank you.'

'So who's the frosty bit of stuff working here? Hal whinged about a stuck-up blonde — he says she gives him a lot of grief.'

Her eyes widened, but she couldn't suppress the laughter bubbling inside her. 'I guess that'd be me!'

'Nah — not a gorgeous lady like you. It has to be someone else. When Hal first met this woman, he decided she was Attila the Hun reincarnated in female form.'

'Is that so?' Zillah's smile faded.

'Yeah, he's a funny guy, isn't he?'

'He cracks me up.'

Zak tilted his head to one side. 'Your name, by the way, would go really well with mine if we formed a double act. Zillah and Zak? Cool, don't you think?'

'I should tell you I was called Killer Zillah at school.'

'I can imagine. My real name's Jack Brown.'

'Nice name,' she said.

'Exactly.' He dismounted from the chair. Shucked off his jacket and looked around.

Zillah indicated a hook on the back of her door. 'So, what exactly has your friend Hal been saying about me — apart from the Hun joke, that is?'

Zak sat down again. 'Just that the two of you had a bit of a run-in. Nothing mega. Mind you, old Hal can be a bit of a nitpicker. Stubborn devil too.'

'Really? Now, that I find hard to believe.'

Zak nodded. 'To tell the truth, he hasn't been the same since Jessie moved in.'

'Jessie being?' She closed down her spreadsheet. It could keep. Who needed soap operas with this going on?

'Jessie's his lady, his live-in girlfriend or whatever.' Zak leaned in. 'I never met her when they lived in London — haven't seen him for ages in fact. My work takes me all over the place.' He rubbed his chin.

Zillah rearranged her pens. 'I assumed he was married. Don't ask me why.' She knew she shouldn't gossip with this stranger, but couldn't seem to stop herself. Zak was incredibly easy to talk to, far more so than Hal. Her throat dried as she realised the probable reason for this. She didn't fancy Zak, was why.

'He looks the settling-down kind, doesn't he?' Zak went on. 'Got that resigned expression.' He put his head on one side, as if considering. 'Unless it comes with the job? Bean counters are generally harbingers of bad tidings, aren't they? Like politicians?'

She laughed. 'So how long is it since you last saw your friend?'

'Fact is, Zillah, I was in Hal's bad books big time after I, um, dumped his sister when she came back from a holiday in Spain. She wasn't exactly heartbroken about ending the relationship, and I probably did her a very big favour. But Hal was like a mother hen about her. Even after all that time, now I need a bit of help from him, I wouldn't mind betting I have to grovel in order to obtain it.'

★   ★   ★

Hal Christmas parked his car in its allotted space and glanced at the dashboard clock. Fifteen minutes late. He swore out loud in German, a language in which he was fluent and found useful when venting his feelings, depending whose company he was in. There was no sign of Zak, though a vehicle was parked in the visitors' bay. If this belonged to Zak Silver, the poor guy was probably prostrate behind the building, his heart pierced by a stake. Zillah's van remained where she'd parked it that morning. The visitor had obviously brought Mrs Robinson to the door. Bad news.

But no wonder she so often came over as prickly. She must still be vulnerable after what she'd gone through. He steeled himself not to feel sorry for her. At least she hadn't been rejected. At once, he felt ashamed at his insensitivity. His pride had been hurt; she'd lost her husband. No contest. He got out of his car and strode towards the building, but avoided glancing in at Zillah's kitchen window. He could do without being struck down by one of her withering looks.

The front door was locked. Hal had a key, but didn't relish ringing from his office to ask if she was holding Zak hostage, so he loped round the side of the building. He knew her section of the premises backed onto a swathe of scrubby land with a fence a maximum-security prison would be proud of. He snuck round the inside of the fence, hoping for a quick glance through the window, which he saw was open at the top. At once he heard Zak's unmistake-able mellow tones. Laughter floated from inside. Hal felt a jolt, the like of which he'd not experienced since Jessie broke the news of her departure.

Zillah was leaning back in her chair, her lovely throat creamy above the neckline of her filmy white blouse. She never relaxed like that with him. He knew he should duck backwards before she noticed him; but she glanced his way, and their gazes locked before her smile switched off, even though Zak was probably still chatting her up. She rose and headed for the door. Hal turned in haste, almost tripping over a discarded tyre. He cursed and decided to tell the truth, say he was trying to find Zak and hadn't wanted to disturb her. That way, she'd think he was a wimp — which was marginally better than being thought of as some kind of weirdo.

★ ★ ★

'So, you plan on being around a few months.' Hal ushered Zak into his office and checked his watch. 'Tell you what, rather than stay here, how about we talk over a drink and some supper?'

'Fine by me. I'm always hungry. What about your gorgeous neighbour?'

'You mean the fair Miss Frigidaire, as the man says in the song? Don't even think about it.'

Zak raised his eyebrows. 'Hey, we hit it off, man. She'd probably love to join us.'

Hal's jaw tightened. 'She's just leaving. Trust me. The woman likes her own space.'

'You're not seriously going to tell me Zillah Robinson really is the blonde who turns you off?'

Hal hesitated. *If Zak only knew.* 'That's the one.'

Zak's eyebrows shot heavenwards. 'She said as much to me, but I thought she was teasing.' He glanced around. 'So, are you pleased to be out of the rat race?'

'Very pleased.' Hal picked up his briefcase. 'But I'm trying to organise my new home as well as this place. Office furniture arrives tomorrow.

That's why I drove back to the cottage earlier — so I could load up files and stuff, ready to unload in the morning. I'm sick of having to move things to make room for other things.'

Zak rattled his car keys. 'Shall I drive?'

'If we take both cars, you can go on to Bristol later. You don't want to have to bring me back here.'

Zak rubbed his chin. 'I was kind of hoping I might be able to crash here tonight.'

'In my office? Whatever for?'

'My mini's a cool motor, but my legs aren't built for back-seat sleeping.'

Hal groaned. 'Don't tell me Kylie's kicked you out again?'

'Changed the locks this time. I got an email before I left Vegas.'

Hal sighed. 'We'll go in my car. You can stay at my cottage tonight, but don't expect the Ritz.'

'You know what, Hal? You're quality.'

'Yes, well, you can pay for the meal. And you better grab your overnight stuff from your car before we go.'

'I'm such a muppet.'

'Not for me to argue,' said Hal. 'Any particular reason?'

'I've just realised my jacket's still hanging in the delectable Zillah's office.' Zak slapped his back pocket. 'Don't worry. I have my wallet. And she has a tangible reminder of me 'til she and I meet again.'

6

Zillah arrived home to find that the gardener had left a treasure trove on the back step. Upon the yellow courgettes, feathery-topped carrots, satin-leafed spinach and waxy new potatoes, Ruby slumbered, maybe dreaming of a tasty supper. Zillah picked up basket and kitten and carried them inside the back door to the garden flat, which doubled as her main entrance. The morning's mail lay on the mat and, taking her cargo into the kitchen, she placed it gently on the floor before pouring water into a saucer to leave beside the basket. There was wine chilling, so, even though it was a weeknight, she poured herself a glass and sat down at the table to gloat over her latest letter from Montreal.

At school in Cornwall, Zillah had been one of a trio of friends. But when the other two decided to apply for university places, Zillah didn't follow suit. Her parents ran a medium-size hotel, and knew she had the catering gene. She was already helping in the holidays and putting aside earnings, and her father chipped in so she could take a course at the prestigious Leith School of Cookery.

The summer of the girls' A-level exam results, Zillah had answered the phone and spoken to a man who said that the Cove Hotel was the sixth he'd contacted.

'I'll never speak to you again if you've put a No Vacancies sign outside,' he'd said in a voice that told her he was smiling.

All she could offer for the next three nights was a small single room with no sea view. 'It has bunk beds,' she'd said. 'In high season, it's normally let to families who only want somewhere for the children to sleep. It's not an en suite, but there's a washbasin and a bathroom just opposite.'

'Fantastic. I'll take it,' he'd said. 'Would you mind if I cover the top bunk with a plastic sheet so I can spread my stuff out?'

'Let me guess. You're an artist?'

'For my sins. I expect you get plenty of those, don't you?'

'We do. What name is it, please?'

'Daniel Robinson. I promise you I'm house-trained. And I may not arrive till sevenish, so please don't give away my room.'

As Zillah replaced the receiver, she wondered why his name seemed familiar. At that moment she remembered that the art teacher who'd seen her through her coursework was a big admirer. Mr Robinson must have decided to make a last-minute trip, and found he was unable to book into any of the smarter hotels.

★　★　★

The restaurant Hal chose for his meal with Zak still awaited the evening

101

bustle, and the two men were shown to a window table. 'So, you've saved lots of money?' Hal tore off a chunk of naan bread.

'Um, sort of.' Zak didn't meet Hal's gaze. 'One-armed bandits don't do it for me. Some of my mates ended up hooked, but I, um, found more entertaining pastimes.'

'I can imagine.' Not for the first time, Hal thought how fortunate it was that his sister had met the man destined to be her future husband before there'd been time for her relationship with Zak to deepen. Nina still suspected the singer of stringing along two other gullible girlfriends apart from her. She'd told Hal that Zak seemed relieved when he dumped her, and she explained she'd been about to tell him she'd met someone else.

'How's Nina doing?' It was as if Zak read Hal's mind.

'Very well indeed. She adores Majorca. She and her husband have three children now.'

Zak bit into a green olive. 'Three kids? Good for them. Does she work?'

'If you mean supporting a busy Majorcan GP, raising three lively youngsters under the age of eight, and maintaining her elderly mother-in-law's garden plus her own, then the answer to your question's yes. Especially if you count juggling.'

'Whoops. Sorry, mate. It's lucky for me you don't bear grudges.'

'I was relieved when you two stopped seeing each other before you could break her heart. I sometimes wonder how much money I'd have spent on therapy if she'd married you instead of Dr Carlos Antonio.' Hal leaned back as the waiter arrived with their food.

'I'm not disputing that. Even I wouldn't want to be married to me.' Zak addressed the waiter. 'Could you bring two more lagers, please?'

'I hope they're both for you,' Hal cut in as the waiter sped away.

Zak blinked. 'I forgot you're lumbered with driving. My turn next time.'

'Zak, if you're planning to stay around, I can't guarantee any work at the moment.'

'Understood, but — '

'My new enterprise is an unknown quantity. What I hope is that people will lash out for their stag nights and corporate events, even if they cut back on holidays and personal spending.'

'Fair enough. Even if you will insist on sounding like a number-cruncher.'

'That's my bread and butter. I can promote you as a singing waiter, wedding singer, or whatever. But please don't hang about in hope of making a living out of gigs I can't offer.'

Zak spooned lime pickle onto his plate. 'Fabulous food.'

Hal cleared his throat. 'This restaurant has been recommended to me by Mrs Robinson.'

'So you do actually talk to one another without snarling?'

'As and when appropriate.'

'Missed opportunity, my friend, even if she's already taken.'

'Fortunately, not all of us share your unprincipled tendencies.'

'Ah. I suppose that's because you're still with Jessie. How's that going?'

'It's not,' said Hal. 'Jessie went her own way many months ago. What you should know is that Zillah's widowed; and not that long ago, either.'

'Wow, oh, poor baby.' Zak leaned forward. 'Appreciate the heads-up, Hal. I wonder if I should offer to take her to lunch tomorrow.'

'I don't think her appetite's a problem.' *Sunday morning sticky fingers.* He remembered how she'd so obviously enjoyed the cakes, licking her fingers afterwards in a rare moment of relaxation in his presence. Why did he feel so irritated by Zak's lunch suggestion? He gulped water and drew one hand across his forehead. The spicy curry tasted fantastic, but he hoped his body's cooling system could cope.

'Thanks for laying it on the line, Hal. About work prospects, I mean. I have a job coming up for the autumn, a West End show this time. And my agent might find me a few gigs. I don't particularly want to live full-time in London while it's summer.'

'Wouldn't your folks put up with you for a while?'

Zak swallowed a mouthful of lager. 'My mother would, of course. As for the old fellow — don't ask.'

'No chance of reconciliation with —?'

'Probably better not to go there. Kylie's a lovely girl and she deserves better than me.'

'Dare I ask if this is a sign of maturity?' Hal snapped a poppadom in half.

Zak shrugged. 'Enough of my love life. This website you mentioned — d'you plan on building it yourself, or will you hire a designer?'

'I haven't given it too much thought. I don't even have a name for my new venture now.'

'I heard about that from Zillah. Tough luck, mate.'

'How does she rate me, compared with pond life?'

'She was the soul of diplomacy. You know, I think I will ask her out to lunch. She must have lots of girly contacts. I could offer my services for hen nights.'

Hal rested his fork. 'Please don't tell me you fancy yourself as a singing strip-o-gram.'

'Needs must — ' Zak's attention wandered as four young women took their seats at a nearby table. A cute redhead, poured into a slinky black silk tube, met his gaze.

Hal watched the master at work. Zak glanced away before the girl did. Then he looked back and smiled just the tiniest smile. The redhead tucked a strand of hair behind one ear before picking up a menu, which shook as she held it. Hal's instinct told him the dishes on offer might have been written in Elvish for all the interest she had in them. He reckoned, not for the first time, that his sister's guardian angel must have been on full alert when Nina went on holiday to Majorca with a girlfriend, leaving Zak allegedly inconsolable in London, a decade ago.

★ ★ ★

Zillah reread the letter from her friend Caroline after she'd eaten a dish of steamed vegetables with grated cheese. Ruby woke, lapped at the saucer of water and leapt aboard Zillah's lap for a cuddle. When she let the little cat out, the other two felines stalked from the shrubbery to claim her. It was like keeping an assignation with someone out on parole.

Caroline was the best correspondent of the three women friends. She rarely emailed, but when she wrote a letter it was worth having. This time she urged Zillah to fly out and visit.

She'd been before, but on both occasions Daniel had been with her. He'd spent most days sketching while Zillah saw the sights. Evenings, the four of them walked, talked, ate and drank, philosophised and laughed. There was always laughter with Daniel around. He'd adored being the only male with three attractive women, insisting upon naming them Daniel's Angels.

'It's you who were my angel, Daniel.' Zillah's words were a whisper. When, oh when, would that gnawing ache subside?

She folded the letter to keep in her handbag. She'd neither the time nor money to take a trip just now. Maybe in a year or two she'd manage to get away. Maybe the three friends should aim for a reunion the year they hit forty. She shivered. Somehow she didn't want to think of that. Being the adored wife of an older man no longer cushioned her from fear of the future. Daniel had been so energetic, so positive. It didn't seem fair.

Her thoughts roved to Hal. He was the first man she'd been affected by in many years. She decided upon an early night. She needed to be at work by eight the next day.

★ ★ ★

'If you want a lift in the morning, you'll have to be ready by eight.' Hal drove cautiously down the narrow track leading to his cottage.

'So be it.' Zak clutched the grab handle over the passenger door. 'I see what you mean about the ruts.'

It was still light but Hal slowed in good time for his gateway. Even after a couple of weeks' residence, it was easy to overshoot. The overgrown hedge bulged at either side of the entrance, the foliage forming excellent camouflage.

Zak whistled at first sight of the cottage. 'Sheesh! It's like something straight from a gothic fantasy. A witch's gingerbread house, maybe. Bring on the hobbits! You've found yourself a cool pad, mate.'

'Yes, well, it was affordable. You'll

understand why, when we're inside. Been on the market a while.'

'Plenty needs doing?'

'Just a bit. I don't care if it takes me years, though.'

'Mr Christmas is planning to put down roots? Something you're not telling me, perhaps?'

Hal unlocked the front door and barged through it. 'This door's only one of the things that needs fixing. And I certainly don't contemplate moving again for a long while. After you, Zak. At least you can walk through to the kitchen now, without falling over boxes.'

'Do you keep late hours?' Zak gazed round him.

'Depends. Why? D'you fancy a nightcap?'

'Whatever. I don't want to be a nuisance.'

'I won't let you be.' Hal pointed to a door. 'That's the kitchen. There's a bottle of Scotch in the cupboard over the sink. You'll have to improvise when it comes to glasses. I'll go and grab a duvet, etcetera. You can use the back bedroom.'

'Then maybe I could run a few more ideas by you?'

Hal loped upstairs, wondering what these might be. He hoped Zak didn't think he could lodge with him indefinitely. He had a fair idea of what that would entail, and he really didn't want the hassle of finding some strange woman standing in his kitchen, rummaging in the fridge for orange juice while her lover finished his beauty sleep.

He surprised himself by quickly locating spare bedding. On his way downstairs he heard the kettle coming to the boil. If Zak was making himself a cuppa, there was hope for the singer yet.

★ ★ ★

Zillah arrived at work next day to find a suite of new office furniture sitting on the forecourt. The silver Mini still stood

112

where Zak had parked it the night before. Head down, she let herself into her premises before the deliverymen could interrogate her, opened her office door and paused. She sniffed. Her sense of smell was good. And this smell was good, too. Top-quality leather. She peered round the door and saw Zak's jacket still hanging from the hook. She decided not to move it, in case she gave the impression of caring what happened to Mr Christmas and his entourage.

She remained undisturbed; and when, a flock of vol au vents later, she returned to her office to check emails. There was one via her website.

Lonely male, separated from favourite jacket, seeks sympathetic female. How about lunch?

Her spirits rose. Suddenly she decided that lunch with an attractive man, even if he was Hal Christmas's buddy, sounded fun.

Zillah typed a reply: *Meet you outside at 1.00 p.m. Some of us have work to do!!!!*

She deleted three of the exclamation marks and pressed Send. But the rest of the morning flew by; and, before she knew it, Zak's hand was cupping her elbow as they left the building. And he smelt divine. She thanked her lucky stars she was no longer twenty.

'How about The Golden Fleece?'

'You're a fast learner. That's my local — well, it is when I'm working here.'

'Hal pointed it out yesterday. Come, lovely lady. My silver Mini awaits.'

'Coincidence,' she said. 'Guess who that silver van belongs to?'

'We're twin souls, you and me. Why fight it?' He zapped his key lock and opened the passenger door.

Laughing, Zillah strapped herself in, and waited for him to get behind the wheel. 'Enough that my street cred will probably quadruple when I walk into the pub with you.'

He chuckled. 'I try. Of course, I realise you're just toying with me.'

She was enjoying herself, feeling totally relaxed with a man, for the first time in ages. 'So, will you be around a while, or are you just passing through?'

'As it happens, I've made a deal with the big guy. He's letting me crash at his place in return for constructing his new website.'

'Where exactly does he live?' She noticed how cautiously Zak navigated the slip road. Probably Hal had warned him how women round here drove straight at the jugular.

'On the Bath side of Bradford-on-Avon,' said Zak. 'In a very quaint but run-down cottage that'll probably turn out to be as high-maintenance as a Parisian mistress.'

Zillah knew she shouldn't ask but failed dismally. 'So, if you're about on the weekend, you'll get to meet his wife — partner — whatever?'

'Flipping traffic doesn't get any better round here, does it? Um, Jessie's no longer on the scene. It took three scotches before His Nibs told me the full story. I asked him if he fancied a blind date tonight but he bit my head off. I can't imagine why.'

'Oh dear.' She was experiencing a strange feeling of relief and longed to hear more, but Zak indicated right and they pulled into the pub car park.

'Lunch on me,' he said. 'No arguments.'

'But Zak, if I pay, I can claim it on expenses.'

'Damn,' he said. 'I knew it.'

'Knew what?'

'Knew you didn't take me seriously. If you did, your tax return would be the last thing on your mind. Come on.'

It is a truth universally acknowledged that, when an attractive single woman turns up at her favourite hostelry with a stranger, an attractive male into the bargain, it's bound to cause comment. Zillah recalled Abi's words as she noticed Mickey smooth down his tie on seeing her.

'Zillah,' he called. 'How goes it? Got that schmuck sorted yet?'

'Um, yes thanks,' she said. How embarrassing was this? Mickey wasn't usually so tactless. What if Hal Christmas had been her lunchtime companion and not Zak? She pushed the thought away.

'What would you like to drink, Zillah?'

'Sparkling mineral water, please, Mickey. This is Zak Silver. He's an entertainer and he's between gigs at the moment.'

Mickey reached over to shake hands. 'Good to see you, Mr Silver. And what can I get you, sir?'

'I'll have the same as the lady, please. And we'd like lunch for two. Zillah tells me the food's great here.'

Mickey flipped the metal tops off two frosted bottles. 'Are you the same Zak Silver that came to Bath in that musical thing a while back?'

'I don't think there's another actor of that name so probably, yes. I'm impressed you remember.'

Mickey placed two tall glasses clinking with ice on the counter. 'My wife dragged me round the stage door to get your autograph afterwards. You weren't too bad if I'm thinking of the right bloke. You still singing?'

'I do my best,' said Zak.

Mickey's pen was poised to write their lunch order. 'That particular wife gave me the sack not long after, if I remember rightly.'

Zillah hastily ordered the crab cakes with salad.

★ ★ ★

'Thanks for waking me last night,' said Hal as Zak stumbled into the kitchen next morning, scratching his left armpit. 'You look terrible. Good job your fans can't see you now. Coffee and toast?'

'Just coffee please, mate. Sorry about last night. I tried not to disturb you.'

'This morning, you mean. And that door would defy even the most tenacious of burglars.' But Hal was smiling. 'I can put up with you for a few nights, I guess. And I've made a decision about this place.'

118

Zak sipped his coffee. 'Sounds ominous.'

'I was planning to do the renovation on my own — take years over it if necessary. Now I'm wondering whether I can tolerate living in a tip as well as running two businesses. Am I totally insane?'

'You're certainly a workaholic. You should try chilling out more. Look at me — '

'I am,' said Hal grimly. 'I hope you were careful with that poor girl last night.'

Zak groaned. 'You have no idea! She invited me back to her place for coffee. Wish I hadn't gone, now.'

Hal couldn't resist asking. 'So it all went pear-shaped?'

Zak spread his hands. 'What a man-eater. I like the build-up to be subtle, not like a rugby scrum. And certainly not the full Monty on a first date — I do have scruples.' He stretched his arms out wide. 'When she went off to the bedroom, I pretended I'd got a text from my agent and needed to drive straight to London.'

'Did she believe you?'

Zak nodded. 'I told her I had an audition first thing this morning in the West End, and daren't risk getting snarled in traffic. She told me she'd like to cook dinner for me at her place next time.'

'You don't seem too happy about it.'

'I know. Pathetic, isn't it? Truth is, mate. I've kind of got a crush on Zillah. Now, there's a real woman for you.'

'Oh, hell.' Hal sucked his finger where he'd sliced it with the bread knife. He turned on the cold-water tap and watched the crimson drops swirl down the plughole. 'Isn't it a bit unkind, moving in on someone still recovering from losing her husband?'

'But I don't intend doing any such thing. What d'you take me for?' Zak looked hurt. 'I enjoy her company and she seems to enjoy mine.'

'How very touching. Where did I put those plasters? Do I even possess plasters?'

Zak got up. 'Thanks for the coffee. Okay if I shower now?'

Hal didn't respond. Just ripped off a sheet of kitchen roll and wrapped it round his finger before stuffing two slices of bread in the toaster. He didn't trust himself to speak.

7

'Yet another beautiful woman in my sights? Be still, my beating heart!' Zak hovered in the open kitchen doorway, admiring Abi in her pastel floral leggings and black shoestring top.

Hal thundered upstairs to his offices, face impassive. 'Morning, Abi,' he called.

'Morning, Hal,' she called back before addressing Zak. 'And you are?'

'Zak Silver.' He held out his hand.

Abi shook it. 'Abi Knight, Zillah's assistant. Are you an accountant like Hal, or are you a fire-eater?'

'Neither. I bend spoons for a living.'

Zillah emerged from her office. Zak turned to greet her, taking her hand and kissing it. Abi whistled.

Hal called down the staircase: 'Hey, Zak! Are you planning on getting started today?'

Zak mimicked slitting his throat with his forefinger. 'See you anon, ladies. Duty calls.'

Zillah shut the foyer door firmly behind her as Abi went off to change into whites. 'There goes an absolute charmer, Abi. Not a man to fall in love with.'

'Are you telling me or trying to convince yourself?'

'I'm merely making an observation. More importantly, we desperately need more petits fours by the weekend. In the mood for marzipan making?'

'You bet. Anyone would think people were eating them. I'll try that no-sugar cupcake recipe as well, if you like. So, do we know what Zak's up to, other than bending spoons?'

'Mr Christmas has asked him to create a website for this new venture of his.'

'So Zak Silver's not just a pretty face.'

'He's also a singer, with an impressive CV — plus a website. I'd never heard of him, but he's done loads of stuff in the West End and on tours.'

Abi puffed out her cheeks. 'Two new men turn up and you've made a hit with each of them. Can't be bad.'

'I don't want to make a hit with either of them, thank you. Quite frankly, I can't think which one would prove the worse proposition.'

'Zak seems fun.'

'Oh, he is. I enjoyed our lunch yesterday.'

'Lunch while my back was turned? Didn't I just hear you say you weren't interested?'

'I'm not a hermit. Just not searching for something I know I'll never find.'

Abi bit her lower lip. 'I'll test that recipe you're wondering about, then mix the marzipan. Okay if I play a CD?'

'Of course. Try the one Zak gave me, if you like.'

'Right.' Abi tried not to smirk.

'I know you're highly amused, Abi. But the guy's just being friendly,' said Zillah. 'Plus, he's probably hoping I'll recommend people to buy the album from his website. Did I say I'm driving to Brassknocker Hill shortly? Meeting Mrs West for a preliminary discussion.'

'This is the lady who's panicking because her original caterers have ceased trading?'

'It is. There's a marquee booked for an early-September wedding. We desperately need this kind of function. I'm only sorry we might profit through someone else's misfortune.'

'You're too soft-hearted,' said Abi. 'It's a hard old world out there, boss, so just you go and do what you do so well.'

* * *

In his freshly-painted first-floor office, Hal sat hunched over his laptop, doing something he knew he did well — while also knowing that most people, on hearing about it, would be attacked by irrepressible yawns.

Zak was concentrating on his own screen. Suddenly, he stood up and stretched. 'I could murder a coffee. How about you?'

'You'll find the kettle and stuff next door.'

'In case you're interested, I'm getting on fine, thanks, Hal,' said Zak. 'I'm calling your new business Johnny No Name for the time being.'

Hal knew he was in the wrong. 'I'm sorry, Zak. I really must sort something soon.'

'Why not ask those two downstairs?'

'I don't think so. Zillah has enough on her plate.' Hal got his head down again. 'Black, no sugar, please.'

'She might be flattered to be asked,' replied Zak. 'Why don't I try?'

Hal counted to ten. 'I'd prefer to choose my own name,' he said, keeping his tone neutral.

There was a knock at the open door. Abi stood there, bearing a plate on which she'd placed two chocolate cupcakes. 'We need these consumer-tested,' she said. 'Any volunteers?'

'You bet,' said Hal, smiling at her as

he rose. 'Zak's making a drink. Have you time for one?' Too late, he remembered Zillah's kitchen was cafetière heaven. He couldn't compete with that.

Abi consulted her watch. 'That'd be great. I was going to make myself an instant in a mo.'

So, the Fair Miss Frigidaire didn't always insist upon freshly-ground. Hal moved a chair forward. 'Come and test-drive my new furniture.'

Zak put his head round the door. 'I thought I heard the lovely Abi. Milk and sugar for you, darling? Luckily, I've found three mugs, though I'd have given up mine for you.'

Abi chuckled. 'Just a splash of milk, please.' She sat down opposite Hal. 'How do you put up with him?'

'Fortunately, he doesn't waste his charm offensive on me.' Hal accepted a cupcake. 'Mmm, this smells good.' He bit into it. 'It tastes good, too. Dark. Rich. Not too sweet.'

She beamed. 'That's exactly like men

should be. Seriously, we're trying out a no-refined-sugar range.'

'You'd never know you used a substitute. This is really good.'

'That's honey with ground almonds, as well as cocoa powder. So, you like?'

'I do. Maybe Zak should let me eat his. He needs to watch his waistline.'

Zak brought in three mugs on a biscuit tin lid. 'There's nothing wrong with my waistline. I work out.' He whipped the other cake out of Hal's reach and bit into it. 'Brilliant. Abi, are you single? I'm on the verge of proposing.'

'On your bike, Mr Silver. I'm spoken for. Anyway, Zillah tells me you're the kind of guy women should steer clear of.'

Zak looked hurt. 'She said that?'

'She's a fair judge,' said Hal. Strangely, the morning had got better.

Zak sat back down. 'Ah, all the more reason to prove her wrong, then. Cheers.' He picked up his mug. 'Where is she, anyway? I'm disappointed she didn't want to take a break too.'

'Zillah's gone out on business. This one's a biggie, if she pulls it off.'

'A wedding reception? My antennae are quivering.'

'Yep. One of those fabulous Georgian villas, with a garden to make mine seem like a window-box.'

'Wonder if they've booked any entertainment,' mused Zak.

Hal was trying not to show his overwhelming relief at hearing Zillah's character assessment of Zak. It showed a level of shrewdness he found impressive. Until it occurred to him that the lovely Mrs Robinson doubtless held an equally scathing opinion of him.

* * *

As Zillah negotiated the traffic, she considered Abi's comment about her lack of ruthlessness. Daniel had been so tender-hearted; maybe it had rubbed off on her. She'd always thought he undervalued his talent. He'd come out of a stormy first marriage when she first met him, the whole business leaving him somewhat insolvent but not embittered. She smiled while she waited for the lights to change. He'd spoken about coming into the light when he fell in love with her. Light was one of the reasons he'd so loved the part of Cornwall where her parents had owned their hotel.

On his first visit, he'd arrived at the reception desk as she calculated a guest's account. The front door was standing wide open and, not noticing him come in, she'd jumped when she heard a pleasant male voice seemingly out of nowhere.

'You're not too fond of computers, are you? I bet you prefer peering into rock pools to peering at a monitor.'

She'd gazed into a pair of kindly eyes set in a tanned face and rose from her seat, something telling her this man was special. How right she had been.

Zillah dragged herself back to the present and slid into first gear. No more

130

daydreaming, and hopefully no road-works to hold her up. She was cutting it fine, and being punctual for a client meeting was important, especially when it was a new one.

When she reached the gated entrance-way, she opened her window to speak into the machine.

'Hang on while I let down the drawbridge,' answered a well-bred young, female voice.

Zillah watched the wrought-iron gates swoosh apart, allowing access to the grounds. She saw lawns like green velvet as the gravelled drive wound towards the imposing villa, its honey stone façade bare of creepers, as if unwilling to conceal any of its lovely features.

'Wow,' said Zillah aloud. 'Even the Nancarrow house could fit inside this place, and then some.' She parked beneath a copper beech tree for luck. Daniel had once been commissioned to paint a beech grove, and the glowing colours still lived on in her mind's eye as well as on canvas.

A man in charcoal pinstriped trousers and an open-neck lilac shirt was bearing down on her, wheeling a barrow. She got out of the van and greeted him. His hair was trimmed as beautifully as the lawns. Did even the gardeners dress to harmonise with the surroundings?

'Good morning,' he said, twinkling at her. 'Are you the one who's going to restore my wife's equilibrium?'

'Um, I'm from *Mrs Robinson*, here to see Mrs West.'

'Mrs Robinson, that was the name Annie mentioned. Follow me, my dear.'

Zillah was about to do so when she realised her 'bible' — containing menus, references and publicity stills — still lay on the passenger seat. She grabbed it and followed the man in the lilac shirt around the side of the house. He parked his barrow at the bottom of a gently sloping ramp, leading to a terrace overlooking not just one lawn, but two. Just like wedding cake tiers, thought Zillah.

The lower lawn appeared to merge into farmland. The view was certainly good enough to eat.

'Annie, your potential saviour's here.' Zillah's guide held out his hand. 'Forgetting my manners. I'm Richard West. Father of the bride, and very much appreciative of your coming to talk to my wife.'

'I hope I can be of help.' Zillah shook hands then turned towards the woman wheeling herself through the patio doors onto the terrace.

Annie West's auburn hair was scooped into a bun, and she wore a pale-blue denim dress and purple Crocs. Her fine-boned face showed she loved the sun, and also cared about her skin, which displayed barely a wrinkle.

'Here she is. My wife, Annie, who's also the one from whom the bride inherits her beauty.'

'What tosh, Richard! Hello, Mrs Robinson. I'm so relieved you could fit us in.'

'Please, call me Zillah.'

'That's a pretty name. Are you Cornish?'

'Yes. I was born there and lived there for years.'

'Lucky you. Shall we talk while I show you my garden?'

'I'd love a closer inspection. Will you trust me to wheel you?'

Richard West smiled at Zillah, and drove his barrow round the back of the house once he'd seen the wheelchair safely down the ramp.

'Two hundred guests don't faze you?' Annie West waited for a reply.

Zillah paused to sniff and admire massed pinks and lavender. Her hand-written notes, dashed off after she'd received the initial telephone call, stated that this meant sit-down lunch for one hundred, and evening finger-buffet for two hundred.

'I couldn't do it minus my loyal team,' she said. 'But I wouldn't dare waste your time if I wasn't certain we could help give your daughter a magical experience.'

134

'Gosh,' said Annie. 'Sounds like you're a girl after my own heart. I've checked out your website of course. But you can talk me through some of the menus, if you don't mind.'

'My pleasure. I love talking food.'

Annie pointed to an archway. 'If you steer through there, we can enjoy the rose garden.'

As Zillah followed instructions, Annie greeted a pretty girl dressed in navy-blue shorts and a sea-green T-shirt. 'This is Chloe. She's my goddaughter and chief dead-header, and we've forced her into slave labour. She needs drinking money for college in the autumn.'

'Tsk, tsk — naughty Godma,' said Chloe. Zillah thought it was obvious they adored one another.

The girl scrambled to her feet and held out her hand. 'Hi. I checked out your website too. I'm a friend of Cara Nancarrow's sister — Cara Maxwell now, I should say. She said your food was yummy beyond belief. Hope

Godma gives you the gig.'

Annie mock-glowered at Chloe, who promptly plonked a kiss on her cheek before checking her watch. 'I'll leave a pot of coffee in the sitting-room, shall I?' she asked. 'I've just remembered Lurch wants me to pick raspberries for lunch.'

'Lurch' is Chloe's nickname for my husband,' explained Annie. 'Our wheelbarrow steers like a deranged supermarket trolley. First time she saw Richard pushing it she came up with the name.'

Zillah chuckled. 'Chloe's lovely. Does he have a nickname for her too?'

'Not repeatable; until you get to know us better, anyway.' She winked at Zillah. 'Now, let's think September.'

'Inside your marquee it'll still be summer,' said Zillah. 'But you might want to choose something sustaining. My menu B features organic sausages for the main course.'

'I adore bangers and mash,' said Annie. 'Excellent blotting paper for bubbly.'

136

'Good. I've taken the liberty of cool-bagging a couple of portions and bringing them with me. You could try them for supper if you like. The gravy contains a magic ingredient.'

'They may not survive 'til supper,' said Annie. 'Now, I have to tell you, my daughter's marrying an Indian science professor. He's delightful, and we couldn't be more pleased with our prospective son-in-law. What we'd like is to combine some of the cuisine of Goa with traditional British. Is that going to be a problem?'

'Not at all. But would you require this theme for the lunch as well as the evening buffet?'

'I think, stay with traditional for the lunch. There'll be some old fogies coming out of the woodwork. How about having a hint of Asian somewhere in the lunch, then going mainly with Indian food for the evening buffet?'

Zillah nodded. 'I've left my folder on the terrace. I'll suggest a couple of starters on the sit-down menu that'd combine well with the bangers and mash. As for buffet food, I already have an Asian cuisine selection you might like to glance through.'

Annie West felt in her pocket and frowned. 'What a pain, I must have left my reading glasses in the sitting-room.'

'Shall I fetch them?'

'Tell you what — why don't we head back and drink our coffee on the terrace? If you go through the French doors, my specs should be on the table in front of the big red settee. They're inside a purple suede thingy.'

Zillah pushed the chair back towards the house, negotiating the ramp with ease. She left Mrs West to pour the coffee and walked inside a sitting-room so vast the gigantic red leather settee looked perfectly at home. She found the specs immediately and bent to pick them up. As she straightened, her eye was caught by the spectacular sunset painted in acrylics and hanging above the massive wood-burning stove — unlit, of course, on such a warm day.

Hot tears stung her eyes. Was this some kind of omen?

Daniel's and her favourite cove, the one not far from her parents' former hotel, shimmered before her. This had been the first painting to receive a red Sold sticker when his work was exhibited in London only months before his death. Zillah was torn. One part of her wanted to kiss the painting. Touch the frame Daniel's fingers had touched. The other wanted to go straight back to Mrs West and blurt out her delight at being confronted by a piece of her late husband's work.

But this would lead to sympathy. Questions. Some people wanted to know how many of his paintings remained in Zillah's possession. Would she ever mount another exhibition? Daniel had worked hard to gain the success he'd achieved, but he'd never hit what people might call the big time. Nor had he wanted 'all that malarkey', as he'd called the trappings of celebrity.

Most of all, Zillah didn't want Mrs

West to assume she was a rich widow, keeping herself occupied by catering for a few functions now and then. Like Daniel, she'd no wish to become a celebrity. But she hungered for business success and needed all the bookings she could get. Zillah drank in the apricot and violet sky above an indigo ocean, and allowed herself two very deep breaths. She mustn't dwell upon the past, even though she wished she could walk into that painting and find Daniel waiting for her. She turned, clutching the purple suede thingy, and went back to Annie West.

* * *

'Sounds like you went down well,' said Abi as she and Zillah lunched later.

'Mrs West promised to ring as soon as she'd made up her mind. Hopefully she'll ask round her contacts to see if they know us.' Zillah remembered the link between Mrs West's goddaughter and the Nancarrow clan. 'I wouldn't mind betting another caterer's being interviewed this afternoon. Which gives me a chance to research some recipes and email my Bath-meets-Goa ideas to her.'

'Brilliant,' said Abi.

'You're prejudiced, but thank you. How's your morning been?'

Abi paused, celery stick in hand. 'I made at least a ton of marzipan. Oh, and the boys upstairs gave the chocolate cupcakes the thumbs up. I thought they might provide some useful comments.'

'Hmm, Mr Christmas certainly has a sweet tooth. I can't imagine Zak being partial to cakes, even sugar-free. There's not an ounce of fat on him.'

'Is that right?' Abi spoke primly. 'I wouldn't know.' She ignored Zillah, about to choke on a mouthful of tuna and tomato. 'They both sampled and both enjoyed.'

'They weren't just being polite?'

'Absolutely not. I had a quick coffee with them before Hal booted Zak back to the computer. He walked me down the stairs, though, and thanked me very nicely for their elevenses. He's such a gentleman.'

'If you say so.' Zillah pursed her lips, put down her fork. 'Sparkling mineral?'

'Thanks.' Abi watched her employer head for the fridge.

Zillah hadn't missed the puzzled expression on her assistant's face, and had a fair idea of what Abi was thinking. It would be along the lines of what a shame it was that Zillah couldn't seem to warm to Hal. Because he was such a lovely guy as well as a gentleman, why would Zillah go out for lunch with a playboy like Zak Silver, when Hal Christmas was far more her type? From her twenty-two-year-old viewpoint, she would reckon Zillah needed someone to help her learn to love again — and sooner rather than later. She shouldn't be wasting her time with Mr Bojangles, fun though Zak might be.

Zillah completed her email to her

prospective client around six p.m. It was a relief to send it winging off, and then to check whether anything interesting had arrived via her website. The only messages were two lonely-hearts ones from Zak.

I'm stuck here. Hal's on a conference call. May I call to congratulate you on your cupcake recipe?

Hey, aren't you speaking to me? Your van's still here. You can't hide from me . . .

Zillah answered the second message, saying she was shutting up shop. Two minutes later, Zak knocked on her door.

'You work too hard,' he said. 'I'm getting a lift back with himself, so I can't offer to whisk you off to the pub. Just wanted to say hi.'

'Hi,' said Zillah.

He beamed. 'Actually, I wondered if you could spare a minute so I can pick your brain.'

'Take a seat. Whether my brain can cope with whatever you need to know is another matter.'

'You're the hearts and flowers expert. Had you thought of asking Hal to promote your business on his website — which, since I am currently constructing it, is destined to be tip-top, state-of-the-art, and so alluring there'll be hit after hit upon it?'

'And your point is?' Zillah regarded him gravely, tapping a tooth with a crystal-topped pencil.

'My point is, it'll mean more business for you. And you do the same for him. Promote the link to his new site as soon as it's up and running.' He folded his arms. 'To tell you the truth, Zillah, I'm hoping to pick up some wedding-singer bookings.'

'I see,' she said. 'How are you on *Panis Angelicus*?'

Zak lifted his chin. 'Just because I've been working in Vegas doesn't mean I don't do serious. I thought you'd visited my website.'

'I have. I'm teasing. You have a fabulous voice, and Abi thinks so too.

We both love your album.'

His face cleared. 'Sorry. It's been a busy day upstairs with God.'

'Zak, listen to me. I'm not that keen on getting into bed with Hal Christmas.' She stopped, aghast at what she'd just said, but Zak didn't pick up on it. 'Our businesses could, I suppose, complement each other; but I find couples often want a disco for the evening party, and have their own ideas as to what's hot.'

'Or cool?'

'Yes. Whatever. I'm sorry, but since I began trading, no one has ever asked me to recommend someone to sing as part of the church ceremony or during the reception.'

Zak nodded. 'I understand. But surely you can see the benefit of marketing your own business via someone else's website? Hal has some good contacts.'

'Not in the Bath area, I fancy.'

'Give him time and I guarantee he'll surprise you.'

Zillah didn't want to be surprised. 'Okay, I'll think about it.' *Anything for a peaceful life.*

That's my girl,' said Zak, relaxing. 'I'd better go upstairs and hover. Hal has so much on his mind at the moment, he's quite likely to buzz off home without me.'

'Are you in tomorrow?'

'Yep. Not sure how much longer the website will take. Once I'm free, I need to go to London and talk to my agent.'

She gathered up handbag and laptop. 'There are three felines needing food, and I have to lock up.'

'Let me relieve you of your things a moment.'

'Thanks.' She was turning the key in the door — Zak beside her, holding her personal effects — when Hal Christmas began clattering downstairs.

Zillah's stomach did its *Hey, we're on a roller-coaster!* routine. She grabbed her things from Zak. Hal nodded at her and stalked out.

8

Crawling in low gear through evening traffic, Zillah had a sudden flashback to the elegant rooms and sumptuous grounds of the house on Brassknocker Hill. Her heart had gone out to Annie West; such a brave and feisty woman. Not once had she mentioned her condition, whatever it might be. Her daughter was still working in Goa. Zillah imagined Lucinda West, maybe wearing a vivid sarong or bright shorts and top, studying *Mrs Robinson* menus on her laptop. Maybe a monsoon kept her indoors at that very moment. Zillah didn't have a clue what the time difference was, but she hoped Lucinda's mother had forwarded her suggestions for the multicultural evening buffet.

Annie had shown Zillah an engagement photo of the happy couple: the fair English rose and the handsome young man. They looked gorgeous enough to model for the cover picture of a romantic novel — maybe one whose title included the word 'sheikh'. Her lips twitched as she wondered what the groom's academic colleagues would make of such a thing.

She drove onto the Honourable Clarissa's driveway, leading to a ram-shackle but useful double carport. As if homing in on any food-related thought, as Zillah padlocked the garden gate behind her, the divas streaked out of nowhere to arrive precisely on cue, purring and weaving around her feet. She bent to stroke each cat in turn. 'No hope of peace until you girls get your supper,' she said, straightening up.

The trio shadowed her as she headed for the utility room entrance. She reached for the cat food and picked up three bowls. Easy stuff, but what would she do about her own supper? Herb-garden omelette, prob-ably, with tomatoes from the greenhouse. Was this how life would be from now on, one solitary meal following another? Did she really want that? Would Daniel have wanted that fate for her? Zillah sighed. It was no use wishing for things to be different. Happiness had been hers once. Now she had to battle solo through the business jungle. Maybe she'd give her parents a long-overdue call.

When she rang, hearing her mother's calm voice made her feel better.

'We were just talking about you,' said her mum. 'How are you, darling?'

'Pretty good, thanks. Busy, but could do with being busier.'

'Tell me about it. Having five letting rooms after twenty-five can be frustrating. Sometimes we could let them twice over, other times we go days without a booking.'

Zillah's folks had sold their seaside hotel and bought a small guesthouse in Wiltshire. They were only a thirty-mile drive from their daughter, but respected her privacy.

'You're a terror, Mum. The whole object of moving was for you and Dad to have a quieter life.'

Her mother chuckled. 'It's hard to break the habit. So, do you have any exciting functions coming up?'

Zillah described her visit to Brass-knocker Hill and the UK-meets-Goa catering challenge. Her mother listened, chipping in now and then.

'You've done your best. They couldn't have better than you. But Zillah, are you busy this Sunday?' Her mother kept her voice casual. 'You could come over for lunch. Let me wait on you for a change.'

'Mum, it's sweet of you, but we're catering a small wedding on Saturday. I might just sleep in on Sunday morning. Then go into work for a couple of hours.'

Her mother's silence was telling.

Zillah sighed. 'It's not as bad as it sounds. And you know how important it is to build good contacts. Someone suggested I might do better by having the *Mrs Robinson* website linked to the website of the entertainments agency that's opened an office above mine. I suppose it makes sense. I'm more interested in making the food right than doing the technical stuff but I really should keep up with my rivals if that's what they're doing.' Zillah didn't mention social media. Abi was happy dealing with that side of things for the business.

'Of course. You always were more creative than inclined towards gadgets. Now, have a quick word with your dad, and if you change your mind about Sunday, just come over.'

It was still only eight o'clock when Zillah put down the phone. It seemed such a waste not to be outside on such a beautiful summer's evening. She could always walk into town and browse the shop windows. Collecting a cardigan, she let herself out of the flat, strolling in the direction of Pulteney Bridge. Whenever she walked across this elegant structure lined with little shops, she wondered what it would have been like back in Jane Austen's day. But she wasn't considering what colour ribbon trimmed Jane's bonnet. It was just too tempting to stop at her favourite café for a glass of wine and maybe one of their luscious desserts. She was highly critical of other people's catering, but this café ticked all the boxes.

The waiter recognised her. 'Busman's holiday?' he quipped.

'Hi Freddie. Can't resist your coffee cake,' she said.

'Glass of chilled Sauvignon Blanc?'

'Why not? I'm walking home.'

He whisked away, leaving Zillah to gaze across the weir. This was another former haunt of hers and Daniel's. His sister had now moved away, but she used to live in the city, and sometimes they'd visit, driving from their home in Cornwall. Somehow Daniel could almost be sitting across from Zillah; his dark, shaggy hair, tinged with silver over the last years of his life, making him even more attractive. He'd loved wearing cords and a checked shirt, always relaxed and blending in, whatever the company.

Often, if they were alone at a restaurant table, he'd reach across and take her hand. Stroke her fingers, running his forefinger around the edges of her almond-shaped nails. He'd loved her to wear nail polish and would sometimes come home with a bottle in a stunning va-va-vroom shade she wouldn't have dared buy for herself. Nowadays, painting her nails was a no-no for Zillah. She closed her eyes for a moment.

★ ★ ★

Hal spotted her as soon as he glanced through the café window. She looked so serene, sitting there on her own, he considered turning round and finding somewhere else to stop for a drink and a snack. But his legs seemed to take on a life of their own and he began to thread his way through the tables.

'Hi. If I'm intruding, I'll leave you in peace,' said Hal, keeping his tone guarded. 'I spotted you from outside, and thought I should come and apologise for my rudeness earlier. I was out of order, but I do worry about Zak's effect on the gentler sex sometimes.'

To his relief, she burst out laughing.

'I'm flattered,' she said. 'But I'm a big girl now.'

'May I?' He gestured to the spare seat. 'Or are you waiting for someone?'

She shook her head.

Hal detected something in Zillah's expression that made him wonder if he'd interrupted a precious memory. The phrase 'treading on eggshells' came to mind, and he felt an overwhelming surge of protectiveness towards her.

'A drink would go down well before I walk back to my car.' He settled himself opposite Zillah.

Her order of wine and cake arrived. 'Would you like to order, sir?' The waiter hovered.

When they were alone again, Zillah couldn't resist quizzing Hal. 'You drive into the city when you want a walk? I thought you lived in the sticks.'

'It's a few miles out from the city, and there's some great walking country, but my living accommodation is less than salubrious at the moment. Hacking my way through packing cases and black bags doesn't leave much chance to explore. I had to come into Bath for a meeting. I happened on this place when I was viewing houses. A stroll down here on an evening like this — well, it's a no-brainer really.'

Hal knew he was gabbling. He didn't add that seeing Zillah was an added bonus. She looked so different now she wasn't wearing a crisp trouser suit, or the *Mrs Robinson* charcoal-and-white uniform. Her gauzy top clung to her curves. Her soft sweater, the colour of smoke and which she wore slung over her shoulders, accentuated those fabulous blue pansy eyes. He didn't like to glance down, but reckoned he'd

155

glimpse a long filmy skirt.

He wanted to kiss her. Wanted very much to run his fingers through that honey-beige hair. He swallowed hard. To make matters worse, above the assorted aromas of roast coffee beans, warm garlic bread and grilled sardines, he could detect a hint of her perfume. He'd learned a bit about scent from Jessie. She'd used something that made a very different statement from whatever it was Zillah wore. The perfume drifting from the woman across the table made him think of Mediterranean nights. Moonlit balconies. Lavender fields a blue haze in the distance. It was, he reckoned, pure Provence in a bottle.

Suddenly, he realised she was ignoring her wine. 'Please don't wait for me,' he said.

He watched her pick up the glass, her hand trembling. The curve of her throat as she held the drink to her lips robbed his breath, his reason. He concentrated his gaze on the coffee machine — or it might have been the menu board on the wall. He didn't know. Because he didn't know what was happening to him.

Or, rather, he did know, but he'd vowed not to lose his heart again. It was never worth the emotional tsunami when the other person backed off. How did anyone capture the art of commitment in such a hectic world?

Somehow, life seemed much lonelier nowadays than it ever did before Jessie. He didn't hanker after her, not since he'd fully accepted how little love there must have been on her side. But he badly missed being one half of a couple. Maybe that was all it was. Come to think of it, he didn't get out much.

Who was he trying to kid? He wanted to reach over and cover Zillah's hands with his own. He mustn't. This wasn't a date. He was sitting opposite this beautiful woman simply because she was too polite to tell him to buzz off. She was a fellow entrepreneur with her own agenda. Hal was only too aware his name didn't appear on that agenda. No way. And why on earth should it?

His filter coffee and dessert arrived. Hal looked down at the soft sponge, coffee buttercream and luscious frosting dotted with dark chocolate beans.

'I can recommend that one.' Zillah picked up her fork. 'I was wondering,' she said, 'about something Zak suggested. Should we perhaps consider publicising our businesses on one another's websites? I know I was less than enthusiastic about your, erm, enterprise when I first heard of it. But, quite frankly, I need all the publicity I can get. And I'm more than happy to reciprocate. Provided,' she said sternly, 'that the entertainers you promote are squeaky-clean.' She ate some cake.

Hal was caught with his mouth full. He reached for a paper napkin. 'Squeaky-clean?'

'As in, no strippers, no dodgy singing telegrams, and definitely no controversial stand-ups. What's so funny?'

He leaned back in his chair. 'You,' he said. 'Do I really look the kind of man who'd know where to find a stripper?'

'No, but I bet Zak would.'

For an instant their gazes met and they laughed together. Then they stopped laughing. Hal leaned forward this time. There was a lot he wanted to say, but somehow the words wouldn't tumble from his lips. He had to clench his fists to stop himself reaching for her hands. Zillah was twisting the sapphire engagement ring on her finger. The ring was white gold, to match her wedding band. Her nails were long and tapering. Beautiful hands. Beautiful woman.

He focused his attention. 'Rest assured, Zak won't be involved in selecting acts. He's on my books as an entertainer. You already know how good his voice is. Meanwhile, he seems to be making an excellent job of my website.'

'Dare I ask what your trading name is? I imagine you've decided by now.'

'Would you believe, *Hal Christmas*? My accountancy contacts know the score, and they seem rather amused by the idea of my wearing another hat.

Anyone wanting to hire an entertainer doesn't need to know I'm a boring bean-counter in my day job. I'm thinking of a database, covering the Bath and Bristol area, so I can offer children's party entertainers, good quality DJs for every sort of function, plus wedding singers. Zak's versatile, and he says he'll be around for the next few months, so I'm happy to promote his singing. After that, he'll be living in London.'

Zillah sipped her wine and picked up her dessert fork again. 'Do you think you two will get on — as housemates, I mean?'

Hal fidgeted with his cup handle. 'Actually, I'm about to tell Zak it's not convenient for him to stay after the weekend.'

'Oh?'

'I had a meeting with a builder earlier. He inspected the cottage yesterday, and it seems one of his clients has pulled the plug on further development, so he can fit me in. He starts work on Monday, and I'm planning to move into a bed-and-breakfast place for however long it takes. It'll be much easier for my builder guy to get on without me tripping over upended floorboards and asking for the power to be left on at night. No way can I leave Zak there. It really wouldn't be safe.'

'I see,' said Zillah. 'So he'll need somewhere to stay?'

'Yes. I've no idea where he is tonight. But if he's not there when I go home, I must have a chat with him tomorrow. I don't suppose you know of anyone with a spare room to let for the next few months?'

Zillah's response surprised Hal. But, he thought miserably, Zak would probably have posed the same question to her on hearing what Hal planned to do.

⋆ ⋆ ⋆

Zillah let herself into her flat, poured a glass of cold water and flopped down at

161

the kitchen table. After Hal insisted on settling both their tabs, and she insisted she was perfectly happy to walk home because that's what she always did, they'd gone their separate ways, Zillah deep in thought. She'd turned round for a last glimpse, only to find Hal standing, staring after her.

She forced herself to think through the practicalities of inviting Zak Silver to rent her spare room. Most of Daniel's painting impedimenta like brushes and palettes, plus ornaments and china and cutlery still in boxes, filled the smallest bedroom. It had always been Zillah's intention to keep the second bedroom free for guests, and potentially for a flatmate. Now, with the possibility of having to deny herself the odd luxuries that helped her through the week, plus fretting whether she could afford an accountant, maybe it was time to do something about it. Clarissa wouldn't mind. She'd gain extra rent while Zillah's own standing order payment would decrease significantly.

But could she share space with a man, especially one she hardly knew? It didn't bother her that Zak was attractive. He was so not her type even if she was in the market, which of course she wasn't. He'd be far too much of a handful. Daniel had been attractive to other women, but he'd been no Casanova. Zillah knew that, since his divorce, he'd put all his energies into his work — until he walked into her life.

She reached for pad and pen. Before she went to bed she'd compile a checklist for Zak. If he agreed to her terms and conditions, he could take over the spare room and move in on Sunday if he wished.

Only then, with a flash of guilt, did she remember the old-fashioned but valuable gold jewellery that had once belonged to Daniel's mother. This was hidden somewhere Zillah considered to be the best place for it. Gold was fetching good prices these days. She pictured the chunky charm bracelet among the items. Her late mother-in-law had been a stewardess for an American airline in the early sixties. Tiny gold aeroplanes and an eagle hung from the chain. If she sold the hoard, she could doubtless keep in with the bank and stop worrying how to economise. She wouldn't have to sublet a room. Yet, somehow, she couldn't bring herself to let go of jewellery Daniel had given her to cherish. Somehow she must keep going. Some day in the future she might be forced to cash in assets like gold bracelets, necklaces and rings.

★ ★ ★

Next morning Hal handed Zak a hand-written envelope he'd found pushed through his business mailbox. The singer's forehead creased as he read the contents.

'Fan mail already?' Hal rummaged in the metal filing cabinet.

'Much better than that. Would you believe, the fragrant Mrs Robinson has invited me to share her flat on a short-term basis? She's offered to show me round after work this evening.' He punched the air. 'Yesssssss.'

Hal tried not to reveal his dismay. So, last night's guarded comment from Zillah about knowing someone who might be interested had resulted in this? What was her idea of flat-sharing? Was the Fair Miss Frigidaire image just an act? How much did she really fancy Zak? His head was spinning and his tongue suddenly felt too large for his mouth.

Zak was scanning the letter. He thrust the second page into Hal's unwilling hand. 'Hey man, how's that for a list? I've got as far as 'washing-machine', and my eyes are glazing over. Does it sound reasonable? Not sure I can tiptoe round all the time.'

Hal glanced down the list until he reached a subheading, underlined by Zillah. Unless she was out at a function, she liked to go to bed early and read. If the wannabe tenant decided to bring someone home, she didn't mind whoever it was staying over occasionally, as long as she didn't use Zillah's toiletries and/or make her late for work by hogging the only bathroom. No way would either Zak or any guest of his be allowed to roam the flat without wearing clothes of some description.

Relief flooded him. Hal couldn't hide his grin. According to these caveats, Mrs Robinson truly didn't appear to have succumbed to the singer's charm. Suddenly, he felt unaccountably happy. But, with a pang, he realised she might be feeling the pressure of financial matters. He yearned to offer assistance but feared for his life.

'Pretty reasonable, I'd say,' he said, handing back the letter. 'Most of it's what most people would do anyway. But you certainly won't be able to watch football matches in your boxers unless your flatmate's working. It's lucky for you most weddings take place on Saturdays.'

'I hope I won't be hanging around watching TV too much. I'm thinking, if I get a gig in the city, I'll be on the doorstep. Save on travel costs. So, what do you think, Hal?'

'I think I should keep out of it. Just don't blame me if it all goes pear-shaped.'

'I shan't let it,' said Zak. 'She's a 24-carat babe.'

Hal caught his breath. 'Don't even think about it,' he snarled.

Zak gave a long, low whistle. 'Does this mean sabres at dawn? You must have it bad, mate.'

'It's not like that.' Hal was lying, flustered by his own outburst, and remembering he'd just said he didn't intend influencing Zak's choice of flatmate. 'I meant Zillah's not inter-ested in another relationship. She's too recently bereaved, and she's still build-ing up her business. The last thing she needs is you plying her with flowers and chocolates.' Guiltily, he remembered the rather enormous peace offering he'd sent. But that had been different. 'Best keep it businesslike if you take up her offer.'

'Hmm,' said Zak. 'I'll certainly go and check it out later. You never know — the two of us might go for a celebratory drink afterwards.'

Hal felt stifled by this conversation. Never mind the sabres; for two pins he'd punch Zak's lights out. Where had that thought come from? He was losing it. Zak was posturing. Zillah, as she had reminded him the night before, was well able to deal with the likes of Mr Silver. But how he wished she didn't act as though he was Mr Ice Man and she needed to out-freeze him. Behind that cool, composed façade was a warm, passionate woman; of that he was certain. He powered up his laptop. Hopefully Zak would have finished working on the website by lunchtime, and Hal's desk would be his own again. What Mr Silver found to do with himself afterwards was entirely his own affair.

★ ★ ★

The tour of Zillah's apartment ended in the kitchen, where it had begun.

'It's a great place,' said Zak. 'Sorry to mess you about and ask to see it in your lunch break, Zillah. I'd definitely like to take up your offer of a trial period.'

'We'll make it three months, if that suits you. You might be able to move back in with Hal — with your friend — after that. His cottage will be habitable by then, I imagine.'

'Nah,' said Zak. 'Hal and I are chalk and cheese. Anyway, I'll be heading for the West End three months from now. Meanwhile, this pad is perfect for me.' He reached for his chequebook. 'The rent seems very reasonable.'

'Good. I'm afraid you'll have to park on the road once our landlady returns, but I'll remind you the day before she's due back. She always rings me.' She glanced at her watch. 'Important to keep things amicable, don't you agree?'

'Absolutely. Now, I can see you want to get on, so I'll just write you a cheque and drop you back at work. I'll go to Hal's place to pick up my gear then drive to my mate's at Clapham. See my agent tomorrow and hang out with some of the guys I know are still in the show. It'll be good to catch up.'

Zillah knew he'd been among the London cast of *The Phantom of the Opera*. She handed him a pen. 'So the Hal Christmas website's up and running?'

'Though I say it myself, it's not bad at all. You can check it out this afternoon if you have time. I think you'll be happy with your link.'

'I'll do that.'

He passed the cheque to her. 'That's to be going on with. You can let me know my share of the extra rent for dual tenancy, and I'll pay you then. I'll be back Sunday evening, unless there's an audition Monday, in which case I'll text you.'

'No need,' said Zillah. 'I understand how your plans might change unexpectedly.' She held out a small bunch of keys. 'You can come and go as you wish now. I don't need to remind you to come in quietly if you arrive in the small hours.'

'I'll try not to annoy you or the divine felines,' said Zak, who was already a big hit with Ruby.

'Please don't give them anything to eat, Zak, even if they hold you hostage.'

He held out his hand. 'You're a hard woman. But let's shake on it. Here's to a happy flat-share.'

★ ★ ★

Back at the office, she told Abi about her new flatmate. 'I'm not sure he's the steadiest person in the world to share with.'

Abi bit into a plump peach, spilling juice down her T-shirt.

At once Zillah ripped off a sheet of kitchen roll. 'Mop it up quickly. Cold water usually does the trick.'

'Sounds like Zak has one foot in London and one here,' Abi grumbled. 'Wouldn't a young professional woman be less hassle for you? Unless there's something you're not telling me?'

'Don't you lot ever give up?' Zillah groaned. 'Hal Christmas was heading for his office just as Zak dropped me off. He looked decidedly, erm, frosty. Honestly, anyone would think I was sixteen years of age — or a scarlet woman. You two are worse than my mum.'

Abi giggled. 'I told you both those guys fancied you. This is going to be very exciting.'

'Abi, you're talking rubbish. This is purely a business transaction, and who I share my flat with is nobody's business but mine.'

'Hey, we care about you, that's all. The fact is, Hal's quality whereas Zak's a serial heartbreaker, and you can do without that kind of hassle.'

Zillah put her hands on her hips. 'For the last time, Abi, I do not fancy Zak Silver. Nor he me.' She paused, closing her eyes, so she didn't notice Abi's face signalling a warning. 'As for Hal Christmas, I wouldn't fancy him if he came gift-wrapped with bells on.'

'Excuse me.' A grim-faced Hal loomed in the doorway. 'I did call out, but you obviously didn't hear.'

If her expression was anything to go by, Hal suspected Zillah wished the ground would open up and swallow her. He guessed his own face must look as though he'd rather be anywhere else but here.

'I'm so sorry,' Zillah gasped. 'What can I do for you?'

'I have a lady here who's just booked a children's entertainer. I mentioned your firm and she's wondering if you can provide a gourmet supper for six, the night of her son's party.'

'Thank you. Thank you so much. I'll take her into my office.' Zillah ripped off her apron. 'I didn't mean what I said just now. I didn't mean you were unfanciable. I just — ' She paused, cheeks reddening.

Hal's gaze took in her trim figure. His eyes met hers. For an instant, electricity so shocking, so powerful in its intensity, crackled between the two. Abi, the spectator, stood open-mouthed. Probably, he thought, she was wondering whether to reach for the fire extinguisher.

To give her due credit, Zillah then greeted her potential client smoothly and ushered the woman into her office, closing the door behind them.

Abi raised her eyebrows. 'What's going on, Hal? Talk about sparks flying.'

'I wouldn't know,' he said gloomily. 'Zillah seems to have reached a very swift decision about Zak. I don't need to tell you he's bad news where relationships are concerned.'

Abi nodded. 'I tease her about him, but Zillah's well aware what he's like. I think perhaps he amuses her. She lets him get away with flirting, but both of them know it's not going anywhere.'

Hal shook his head. Slowly. 'Is that right? Whereas I seem only to infuriate her.'

'I think she's worried about finances,' said Abi. 'She mutters a lot when she's studying her spreadsheets. I wish you two — '

Hal held up his hand. 'No. Please, Abi! Don't go there. Your boss would eat you alive, and follow up with me for afters.'

Abi's chuckle was infectious. Hal laughed too. But inside, he hurt. It was worrying on three counts. Firstly, he hated to think of Zillah struggling without someone to help share the burden. Secondly, he detested the thought of her sharing cosy kitchen suppers with Zak, platonic though their relationship might be. Thirdly, Hal had an awful suspicion he was falling more and more in love with a woman who clearly didn't even like him. Let alone fancy him. Even if he came gift-wrapped.

9

Hot daytime melted into sultry evening. In bed, Zillah counted vast numbers of fluffy sheep. When she did drop off, she woke suddenly, feeling hot and sticky. In desperation, she slipped out of bed at one a.m. and went through to the kitchen in her nightie, a beautiful wisp of honeysuckle silk given her by her late husband. She'd have to remember to put on a sensible robe once Zak was in residence. But she was determined not to object if he wandered between his room and the bathroom clad only in a pair of boxers. She wasn't that paranoid, nor even strait-laced — even if she preferred him to regard her as such.

Zillah dunked a peppermint teabag in a mug of hot water, trying to figure out her feelings. Very aware of her personal security, she always kept the connecting door through to the utility room locked, even though the garden gate was secured too. But tonight she needed to be outside for a while.

She moved cautiously, in case she disturbed any of the cats. Outside, a huge moon reminded her of a beautiful, fragile dinner plate. Zillah sat down on a wooden bench beneath a jasmine bush and breathed in the night scents. She placed her mug of tea on the grass beside her feet just in time. Ruby, returned from some jaunt or other, catapulted on to her lap, whirring like a wind-up toy.

'Hello, scamp,' said Zillah softly. 'I won't ask what you've been up to.'

She sat, stroking the kitten, wondering why things had to be so difficult. She didn't mind working hard. That was a must when running a business on a shoestring. But why, when she'd been so very much in love with Daniel — had been devastated when he was diagnosed with an inoperable brain tumour — why did she now feel so unwound by Hal Christmas?

'I don't want anyone else in my life, Ruby,' Zillah whispered. 'At least, I don't think I do. It's too soon, surely? Yet, sometimes when I look at Hal and he's looking at me, it's like I want to rush into his arms. It worries me, Ruby. I think that's probably why I came out with that nasty remark about not fancying him. Trying to convince myself. I also think the reason why I find Zak such easy company is because I'm not attracted to him like I am to Hal. Anyway, Zak's totally barking. And he'll probably be as charming to the Honourable Clarissa as he is to Abi and me, not to mention the waitress at The Golden Fleece, or somebody like Lady Gaga. He just can't help himself. You know that, don't you?'

The kitten yawned and leapt from Zillah's knee, making for the cat flap and her comfortable bed. Zillah picked up her mug and sipped, gazing at the moon. 'So what does all that tell me?' The question was addressed to no one in particular.

Next morning at seven, having slept all of four hours, Zillah forced herself to focus. She was already at work, spooning creamy curried chicken into puff pastry cases. A bowl of her special spicy prawn filling waited in the fridge. The only trouble was, she kept seeing Hal's face. It was a perfectly pleasant one as faces went, but it didn't help her concentration, especially as this task demanded a steady hand. That awful faux pas yesterday when he'd been trying to introduce new business — how would she ever talk her way out of that one? Hopefully he wouldn't be around today.

Abi arrived well before her agreed starting time of half past seven. She yawned as she came through the door. 'Ooh, sorry, Zillah. Morning!'

'Are you all right, Abi?' Zillah paused, the spoon she was holding suspended in mid-air.

'Hey, watch you don't drop any. I'm

good, thanks. Woke at five and just couldn't go back to sleep. Left Joe still in the land of Nod. Shall I start on the bridge rolls?'

'Please, Abi. One hundred and fifty — smoked salmon, egg mayonnaise, and roast beef with horseradish.'

'Good job my maths is decent,' Abi called over her shoulder on her way to get changed. 'Heard anything more since you emailed your new menu suggestions?'

'About the West wedding? Not yet. As a matter of fact, I'd temporarily forgotten it.'

Abi made no response. When she emerged, on her way to split and spread bridge rolls, she stopped as if wanting to say something.

'What?'

'You. It's so unlike you not to have everything simmering at the top of your cranial list of priorities.'

Zillah burst out laughing. 'Good grief, Abi, you make me sound like some sort of robot. I hope I don't come over as too much of a workaholic.'

'I didn't mean that.'

Zillah's mobile, which she'd left on the draining board, began buzzing like a frenzied wasp.

She peeled off clinging latex gloves to answer it. '*Mrs Robinson*. Good morning.'

'Annie West here. Good morning to you.'

'Heavens, you're an early bird. How are you?'

'Love this time of year, Zillah. Can't get enough of it.'

This, Zillah felt, sounded promising. Unless, of course, Annie was softening her up prior to giving bad news.

'You did say you were catering for a wedding today, so I didn't want to risk one of the guests nabbing our date. Fortunately my daughter got back to me quickly — she and Ravi love your menus. We're all in agreement. We want you to cater the wedding. If that's still okay?'

'Okay? That's wonderful. Wow — thank

you very much for this.' Zillah paused. 'By the way, Mrs West, I wouldn't have accepted another booking for that Saturday without checking with you first. Not even if Prince Harry had asked me to cater for his marriage to, erm, to the Celestial Princess of Ranjapor.'

Annie laughed. 'Now, that would be an exciting opportunity. You deserve the business, Zillah. Between you and me, I did interview another caterer. Their quotation was way above yours, but that's not the real reason I chose you.'

'Uhuh. In your place, I'd have done exactly the same. Food's such a wonderful way to celebrate a happy occasion. It says such a lot. How much you care about Lucinda, how much you value your family and friends being there to celebrate with you. And not forgetting your wish to welcome Ravi into your family. This isn't just a wedding party, it's a celebration of two cultures uniting. You can rest assured the food will reflect love and joy.'

She wondered why she felt a little

choked up. But she wasn't the only one. Down the line, she heard Annie West sniff and clear her throat.

'Thank you, Zillah. I know we've made the right choice. Look, I won't keep you now. Next week, maybe you'd put your quotation in writing?'

'Of course. Have a lovely weekend. I'd like another meeting soon, if that's all right. I'll need to know the size of the marquee, where the comfort stations will be positioned — table sizes, etcetera.'

Zillah ended the call and performed a little dance of joy, ending it abruptly as she saw Hal Christmas passing her window, on his way into work. Thump, thump, went her flibbertigibbet of a heart. Their eyes met as he glanced in. She brushed away a tear, impatient with herself for showing her emotions, and annoyed with him for happening along just at that moment. Wasn't it a bit early for number-crunching? Or maybe he was waiting to brief a team of acrobats and clowns on their way to a garden fête.

Hal stopped in his tracks and nodded. Zillah nodded back. Neither of them smiled until Abi appeared beside Zillah and waved, making his face light up. He waved back.

'You see? He's like a moth to a flame.'

'Nonsense. Anyway, you've certainly made a hit with Mr Ice Man.' Zillah reached for another pair of disposable gloves. That curt nod he gave her had spoken volumes.

'I really don't get it,' said Abi. 'You and him, I mean. He's so easy to talk to.'

'It must be chemistry, I suppose — or the lack of it. We don't seem to be on the same wavelength. Oh, it's no problem being civil to one another over a cup of coffee. But I've probably made the situation even worse now he's heard me telling you how I don't fancy him. Or Zak. Or anyone.'

'Hmm. You certainly seem to find

Zak easier company. I can't think why.'

'Never mind him. I have some good news.'

Abi's fingers flew. 'Business or pleasure?'

'Business, but it's pleasurable too. We're catering the West wedding in September. That was the bride's mother on the phone.'

'How fantastic. Now, that is a triumph. What a biggie! Well done you.'

'As I keep telling you, this is all about teamwork. Without you and people like Jake and the others, I wouldn't be able to take on such a big event.'

'Do they want a wedding singer, I wonder?' Abi's fingers kept flying.

'Are you doing Zak's publicity as well now?'

'I just think he's got such a great voice. I'd want him singing at my wedding.'

'Well, if you get married in the next few months, I'm sure he'd be delighted to oblige.'

The corners of Abi's mouth drooped.

'Joe wants to. Get married, I mean. I'm not so sure.'

'Not sure about Joe? Are you kidding me?' Zillah hadn't quite resumed her former rhythmic drip-feeding of fillings into pastry cases.

'I meant I don't have a great yen for marriage. Yet. Nothing against it. I just feel, well, if something isn't broken, don't fix it.'

Zillah nodded. 'Everyone's different. You might change your mind later.'

'As long as Joe doesn't!' Abi's expression showed how much she cared for her partner. 'He's lovely. We're so lucky. To have found each other, I mean. And I think you're right about the commitment thing. We're trying to save for the future, but it's not easy.'

'No,' said Zillah quietly. 'Life isn't easy, Abi. Now, I must crack on. You're putting me to shame.'

★ ★ ★

186

Hal was checking out his new website. Zak, with his eye for detail and colour, certainly put him to shame where design was concerned. Anyway, Hal was feeling a little guilty about the whole Zak and Zillah business. Hell's teeth, but that sounded like a double act. Move over Wallace and Gromit — here come Zak and Zillah. If *Mrs Robinson* was on shaky financial ground at the moment, its harassed proprietor deserved all the help she could get. Hopefully, much of Zak's verbal leering was just macho chest-beating.

He followed the link to the Zak Silver website and clicked on the Play button to allow the singer's velvety tones to drift through the speakers. This fellow could string the notes together all right. Hal had forgotten quite how good Zak was. Maybe it would be worth contacting the local radio station, see if they were interested in Zak Silver's being back in town. He was, after all, almost a local boy. No harm in reminding people of his existence. It would also keep Hal's mind off Zillah. He hadn't wanted to behave like a lovesick idiot, waving and smiling at her through the glass pane, especially after that acerbic comment he'd heard her make yesterday.

With Abi it was different. She reminded him a little of his younger sister Nina. Consequently, he found her easy company. But when he'd greeted the young woman that morning on his way in, he was very conscious of how it must seem to Zillah. She'd moved away before he could do anything about it. What was it about that woman that transformed him from a hard-nosed businessman into a gauche adolescent with stars in his eyes? Stars that had no business being there.

★ ★ ★

'I began to wonder whether one or two of the guests were going to eat the table decorations,' Abi commented as Zillah drove them back from the function, later that day.

Her boss chuckled. 'Yes. There's a fine line between wanting them to appreciate the food and worrying about having a mountain of leftovers.'

'As if,' said Abi. 'I've never, ever seen that happen.'

'I think it would shatter my confidence if it ever did,' said Zillah, slowing down for an approaching horse and rider. They were a couple of miles outside the city boundary.

'It's not going to happen,' said Abi. 'Do you want me to stay and help wash up?'

'Definitely not. It's Saturday afternoon. You've worked eight hours. I think Joe deserves your company, but thanks for the offer.'

'Okay then. If you're sure.'

'I'm sure. I like Saturday-afternoon radio.'

Abi stayed silent before changing the subject. 'That was a wedding on a shoestring, wasn't it? It didn't seem to matter. The atmosphere was brilliant.'

'The bride's dress came from Monsoon, apparently.'

'Really? Well, she looked like a goddess. If I ever do get married, I shan't be wearing designer stuff.'

Zillah hummed a few bars of a song as she slowed down again, this time for an imaginative maze of traffic cones.

'What's that tune you're singing?'

'Abi,' Zillah sighed, 'I'm showing my age. My mother used to play it a lot — the Frank Sinatra version, anyway. It's called *Love and Marriage*. The two are supposed to 'go together like a horse and carriage'.'

'Ha ha. Maybe Joe's and my wedding carriage is held up on the motorway.'

Abi was so lucky, thought Zillah. So fortunate to have it all in front of her. They drove on in silence, the road descending towards the beautiful city spreading its skirts in the sunshine.

When they pulled up in front of their premises, Zillah was grateful for her assistant's help in unloading the van.

But she was quite content to be left alone to wash up plates and wipe out the cool-boxes. A reception for fifty guests was very different from one for two or three hundred. She'd need to line up her staff well in time for the wedding on Brassknocker Hill. Fortunately, the students on her books would still be on holiday in early September. What a coup it was to have copped this booking. Mr West, a former Member of Parliament, must have loads of important contacts. With her kind of business, spreading the net wider was always on her mind.

Zillah worked on, Radio 4 playing in the background. Abi and Joe would be at the club playing tennis now. Zillah hadn't played for ages. Well, she wouldn't be watching much Wimbledon this year, for sure. The highlights would be all she'd manage, no doubt. Daniel hadn't shared her love of tennis, but never tried to stop her watching. He'd sketched her once, anxious expression on her face, wringing her hands while she watched the British Number One serving for the championship.

'You wear your heart on your sleeve, my darling,' Daniel had said. She could hear him clearly in her head. She still had that drawing somewhere. One day she really must go through all his possessions. Maybe when the wedding season was over. Guiltily, she thought how disorganised she was over some personal things.

After she'd stowed away the rubbish bags, she washed her hands and checked the already-spotless kitchen. Next week so far was destined to be an ominously quiet one. She had bookings for a children's swimming party and a barbecue, both venues in the city. The barbecue was to take place in the garden of one of the houses in Bath's Royal Crescent. The couple wanted steaks and chicken, marinated and delivered for cooking by Zillah's team. There was a list of salads and speciality breads, plus desserts to die for. Jake was to take charge of the bar.

Zillah stopped herself from thinking ahead. She knew she should try to relax more. It was only six o'clock. Maybe she'd call in at The Golden Fleece on her way back to town. They shouldn't be too busy at this time of day, and she could enjoy a long drink with lashings of ice and hopefully catch up with Mickey before heading home. Her landlady's friendly gardener was in charge of the feline trio's supper today, so there was really no need to rush back.

If only that wasn't the case.

10

'Well, look who's here! I bet you've had a hard day. What can I get you, lovely lady?'

Again, Zillah couldn't help noticing how Mickey fidgeted with his tie as she walked towards the bar. Trust Abi to have picked up on that one. She smiled at her host. 'A white wine spritzer please, Mickey. Heavy on the ice and soda.'

The landlord selected a tall glass.

'Busy weekend?' Zillah climbed on to a barstool.

His long, lugubrious face brightened. 'We're fully booked for meals tonight. And I've taken a bed-and-breakfast booking that's open-ended.' He dropped ice cubes into the glass. 'That chap that stole your name for his entertainments agency.'

'Ah, yes,' said Zillah. 'His cottage is

being renovated.' She made a mental note to avoid the pub for the next week. It was a pity, but she really didn't want to fraternize more than necessary. For his sake as well as hers.

Mickey topped up a generous measure of his house white wine with soda, added an ice cube and curly green straw, and placed the glass before her with a flourish.

'Allow me to pay for that. And I'll have a half of that guest ale you recommended, please, Mickey.' The voice was masculine. And familiar as well as very determined.

Zillah didn't have to swivel round on her bar stool to know who stood behind her. Tingles ran up and down her spine in far too delicious a manner. *Help*.

'Thank you, but you really don't have to pay for my drink,' she said.

'I know.' He gestured to the empty stool next to hers. 'May I sit here? Unless you're waiting for someone to join you?'

'No. I mean, yes, you can sit there.

I'm not meeting anyone. I'm on my way home from work.' *Drinking alone. Sad woman.* Why did he have to turn up once again when she was unescorted? Not that she had a string of escorts at the ready.

Hal Christmas, immaculate in cream chinos and kingfisher-blue polo shirt, hooked one long leg around the vacant stool and seated himself disturbingly close. The faint tang of aftershave seemed like coming home now. He looked fresh and very laid-back. Whereas she felt like anyone would feel if they'd worked a ten-hour day and needed a long drink followed by an even longer shower. She disliked feeling at a disadvantage. If he was Mr Ice Man, then why not call her Mrs Limp Lettuce?

'I apologise if you feel I'm muscling in on your local,' Hal said. 'Cheers.' He raised his glass.

'Cheers. Don't be silly, it's the obvious answer for you. Mickey's pleased. Anyway, I'm not in here that often,' she said. *Stop sounding so defensive.*

'No, I didn't mean anything — well, you know — ' His voice tailed away.

She watched him take a swallow of lager. Bent her head over her glass to drink through the silly green straw so thoughtfully provided by Mickey. Fifteen-all, she thought. But somehow her suck turned into a slurping gurgle. She coughed hurriedly and stole a glance at Hal, who she strongly suspected was trying not to laugh.

'I wish we could start again, Zillah,' he said softly. 'I mean, become friends rather than people constantly watching their backs.'

She discarded the dreaded straw and sipped her drink demurely. 'I don't know what you mean. Whatever gave you that impression?'

Hal picked up a cardboard coaster and flipped it edgeways on the bar so it landed back on the counter again.

'Any more party tricks?' She shook her head. 'I'm sorry. We keep snapping and snarling, don't we? It's my fault.'

'Hang on! I upset you first, by pirating your trading name. That was hardly the ideal foundation for a friendly relationship, and for that I've apologised. I believe our two businesses will complement one another perfectly. Sorted. Wouldn't it be better if we could, well, socialise sometimes maybe?'

'I really don't have much time for socialising.' Irritatingly, he'd managed to bump into her twice now outside working hours, and each time he'd caught her on her own. Now she'd succeeded in sounding like Goody Two Shoes. Great.

'Except maybe with Zak?' His tone was teasing but she noticed his jaw clench as he reached for his glass.

'You're worse than Abi. Zak and I have a purely business arrangement, not that it's anyone else's concern. You're not able to put him up in your cottage any longer; I've been contemplating a flat-share. Sorted.'

He ignored the gibe. 'Aren't you and I fellow entrepreneurs? Zak, for all his sins, has reminded me of how important networking is. Don't you, for example, have a florist you recommend if one of your clients enquires?'

His eyes were twinkling. She sipped her drink. Despite the deluge of ice and soda, the white wine was relaxing her, and she thought of the beautiful flowers he'd sent after his 'Mr Robinson' faux pas.

'Well, of course,' she said. 'It's just that I'd never thought about the entertainment scene as such. I can't imagine myself pushing wedding singers and DJs. Clients normally sort that kind of thing out for themselves. Just as they don't normally need help finding a hairdresser or a nail technician, or — '

'Point taken. That girly stuff comes naturally to the bride and her entourage. All I'm saying is, with your local knowledge plus Zak's contacts, between us we'll have access to high-quality entertainers, florists, wine merchants, wedding car suppliers and other specialists. People lead busy lives. They want to be sure of value for their money. With a little lateral thinking, we could provide a competitive and comprehensive service. I don't really have to go on, do I?'

She wished he didn't smell quite so delicious. She probably smelt of eco-friendly washing up liquid. 'Where's this leading, Hal? I don't want too much stuff on the *Mrs Robinson* website. My business is about providing good food. I want people to focus on my menus. I haven't the resources to put myself forward as a wedding planner.'

'Understood. But you're out and about a lot, Zillah. I know Abi's around some of the time while you're meeting clients, but I shall be on the premises most days. Why don't we set up some sort of reciprocal phone-answering scheme? I hate to think you might miss the chance to quote for a function by being out of the office. Could you not trust me a tad more than you do at the moment?'

His eyes were kind. She looked away quickly. How could she think straight unless she did? Maybe she was being too hard on him after all. In spite of her caustic comments to Abi — about clients being put off by being asked if they'd like to book an after-dinner speaker, when they really wanted a luxury picnic hamper to take to the racecourse — his suggestion made sense. Women, especially, would enjoy the sound of his dark-brown voice when they rang up.

Hal Christmas might not be able to sing like Zak Silver, but he could certainly charm the birds out of the trees when he chose — although not usually when it came to her. She was very aware that sometimes, even though her answerphone had kicked in, some callers didn't leave a message. Maybe Hal was right, and they were put off by not being able to speak to a human being. The more she thought about it, the more sense it made.

She stopped fidgeting with her twirly drinking straw and locked gazes with him again. 'All right, Hal. I'll agree that we give it a trial. But you'll have to sort out the techie stuff. Keep me informed as to what expense you incur, and I'll let you have my share.'

He went on gazing at her. This time she didn't avoid his eyes.

She didn't know exactly how it happened, but all of a sudden they were shaking hands and he was asking her if she'd eaten. She'd finished her drink and knew she needed food. A meal with Hal on an otherwise lonely Saturday night seemed very tempting.

'I've booked myself in for bed-and-breakfast from tonight onwards,' he said. 'I wonder if we could have a bite to eat here.'

'Mickey told me he has a full house tonight. I'm sure he'd sort something out for us, but I don't like to presume on his generosity.'

'Quite right,' said Hal. 'I don't want

to start off on the wrong foot. Again.'

He sounded rueful but she didn't want to spoil the moment.

'I live near the city centre. 'There's a pizzeria I know that's not usually busy until eight or so — if you don't mind pizza or pasta.'

'I'm definitely a pizza man. Why don't you leave your van here and let me drive?'

She hesitated. This was becoming a little too intimate. 'I'm not over the limit, in case you're wondering.'

He held up his hands. 'Okay, fine. Do I follow you, or what?'

She considered. He was bound to have to ferry Zak back to her place some time soon. It wouldn't hurt if he knew where she lived. 'It's only a mile or so to my flat. You'll be able to park outside at this time of day, and we can walk into town. Would you mind if I freshened up first?'

'Of course not, but it isn't necessary, surely?'

She laughed. 'Oh, I think it is. I like

my uniform, but enough is enough. You can sit in the garden while I get ready.'

They drove off in convoy. Hal found a parking space just down the street, and she unlocked the side-gate and pointed him towards the bench under the heady white jasmine. It was an evening made for relaxing in the open air with a drink in hand.

'Would you like a glass of Zak's lager? He seems to have stocked up the fridge.'

Guiltily, she remembered her instructions to Zak about not nicking each other's food and beverages. What the heck! Sometimes rules were made to be broken.

'That sounds good,' he said. 'Shall I come and collect it?'

She left him to pour his own beer and hurried off to shower. She wasn't bothered about her make-up as long as she could brush her hair and slip into something cool. She chose a crinkle-cotton dress, its colours shifting from deepest emerald at the bodice down to palest pistachio at the hem. A little black dress or linen sheath might make him think she was keen or something. This was just a meal with a colleague, or almost-colleague, she told herself. On her way back, it seemed silly not to be sociable by pouring herself a glass of chilled white wine.

Hal was enjoying a visit from Ruby when Zillah joined him. 'I see you've met one of the divas,' she said. 'Ruby adores men. You watch the little minx — she'll totally ignore me when I sit down.'

Hal, stroking the kitten, chuckled as Ruby turned her back on Zillah and purred contentedly, digging her claws into his chinos.

'You fickle creature,' said Zillah. 'Who is it that feeds you and talks to you when Roxy and Velma won't let you play?'

'Are you talking about children? I hope you don't mind my asking whether you have any.'

She shook her head. 'Roxy and Velma

are my landlady's other cats. I have no children, and my landlady's are all grown up with kids of their own. Now, we mustn't delay too long, or we'll end up having to ring for a takeaway.'

Would that be so very bad? She'd find it disturbingly easy to stay here with him beneath the jasmine in the velvety, perfumed evening — safer by far to head towards the bright lights.

★ ★ ★

By the time they were seated at a window table in the little restaurant Hal told her he hadn't realised existed, tucked away as it was down an alley, they were chatting more easily. Although Zillah thought he might still be wary of asking what had brought her to Bath, probably not prepared to risk spoiling this unexpected truce in their somewhat stormy relationship. They were both considering the menu. Except Zillah, who knew so many menus off by heart, was experiencing difficulty in concentrating upon types of pizza when the man who so often occupied her thoughts was seated opposite.

'I'm going to order a bottle of white wine,' he said. 'Which one would you prefer?'

'I can't drink a whole bottle on my own. And what about your car?' She bit her lip, afraid she sounded reproving.

'If you've no objection, I can leave it where it is and get a cab back to the pub. Collect it tomorrow.'

'That's fine by me.'

Zillah, despite her wish to keep things on a non-personal footing, soon found that her financial concerns came spilling out. Hal began asking the kind of questions she realised an accountant needed to ask, which she answered to the best of her ability. His gentle interrogation didn't seem too unpalatable while they were drinking such delicious chilled Chablis.

They were halfway through their pizzas when Hal put down his cutlery and picked up his wineglass. 'You know,

I'm happy to give your accounts a once-over. I can tell it's not your forte — and why should it be? You cook like an angel. You also have a genuine flair for presentation.'

'My late husband made a similar comment at our first meeting. But I really can't presume on your generosity. As for the lovely compliment, have you actually tasted anything I've cooked, Hal?'

He leaned forward. 'Your assistant sings your praises. You obviously have the right attributes to help *Mrs Robinson* succeed. I just wonder whether you're operating it efficiently enough, whether you're charging out your time and your helpers' time properly. From what you say, it seems you've built in a realistic profit margin on the costs of ingredients, fuel, etcetera, but I'd need to spend more time on the figures. There's no question of any fee, Zillah.'

'But you're in business to make money too.'

'If it makes you feel better, I'm happy to accept the odd cupcake for my elevenses. More than happy, in fact.'

She sighed. 'I've been whingeing. I'm sorry. I don't usually.'

'When would be convenient for me to make a start?'

'I was planning on tackling my spreadsheets tomorrow morning,' she said. *Wow, how sexy was that?* 'Not too early, of course. But you won't want to be in the office on a Sunday, surely?'

'I need to collect my gear from the cottage and come in anyway. I might as well get some lunch at the pub. How about eleven o'clock at the office? If you'll allow me, I'll copy over your figures so I can access them on my PC. That way, I won't be in your hair for long.'

She nodded. He poured more wine into her glass and she didn't protest. 'Thank you very much,' she said. 'Could I at least pay for supper?'

'Sorry,' he said, topping up his own glass. He tapped his left ear. 'I couldn't hear that last remark. I really can't tell you how much I'm enjoying your company, Zillah.'

'It's not too often I get to eat dinner with someone else. Unless it's Ruby, of course.'

As soon as she spoke, she sensed the change in the atmosphere. Sensed her words had touched Hal. And when she looked into his eyes, she encountered an unexpected and overwhelming sugar-rush of tenderness. It was as though he, as well as she, longed to reach out a hand to the other lonely soul across the table; but neither would reveal their feelings.

Hal, as if he felt it safer to discuss Zak and the possibility of finding the singer some work, mentioned his thoughts about contacting the local radio station on his behalf.

'That's a great idea,' Zillah said. 'I'm sure he'd appreciate any publicity you can organise.'

She'd made the mistake of looking at his mouth. This was a no-win situation, and she felt as if all the breath was squeezed from her body. She thanked her lucky stars when Hal saved the moment by picking up the menu again.

'How about some pudding?'

'I daren't — not after that cartwheel of a pizza.'

'Not even a scoop of vanilla ice cream topped with a little Strega?'

'How decadent can you get, Hal Christmas? Ice cream and Italian liqueur — I so wish you hadn't put that in my mind.'

The waiter hovered. 'Two vanilla ices with Strega, please,' said Hal.

Zillah didn't argue. 'We'll be staggering home,' she said.

'We can hold one another up,' said Hal.

She couldn't help noticing his facial expression, which showed he realised he'd made a crass remark. He hastily asked her if she could recommend a dentist to register with. Then: 'Sorry, Zillah! Not the most appropriate remarks for a dinner date.'

She found it difficult not to giggle.

'Not that this is a date, of course. I, um, I realise that. Sorry. I'm digging myself deeper into a hole.'

'Here come our desserts,' she said, marvelling at the way their pent-up emotions of the last few weeks were being expressed.

'I don't normally indulge myself like this,' said Hal.

'Nor me. It's positively sinful.'

'Isn't it?'

She wondered if he'd suggest having coffee here? If he didn't, would she feel obliged to offer to make some at her place? She'd forgotten how awkward a first date could be. But this wasn't a date. It was, she reminded himself again, a practical conclusion to a business discussion set in motion by a chance meeting.

Hal seemed to have gone a bit silent. How awful if he dreaded her asking him back for coffee. Perhaps she should suggest they book a cab, then the driver could drop her off and take Hal back to

Mickey's pub. That would be safer than strolling home together, their hands so close they might as well be touching.

'Would you like coffee?'

Zillah took a big breath. 'I don't think I can manage it, thanks.'

Hal signalled for the bill and reached inside his jacket pocket to produce a big, soft leather wallet.

'I'll just visit the washroom,' said Zillah. 'Maybe ring for a cab?'

'Yes, of course. The waiter's sure to know a firm.'

'Don't worry, I always use the same people,' she said.

When she returned, they drifted outside. The tables were filling up now. Instinctively, Zillah moved closer to Hal as a group of boisterous young men surged down the street. They didn't mean any harm, and she thought they were just out having a good time, but Hal put his arm protectively round her shoulders.

Somehow, without her knowing how it happened, he had both arms around

213

her and she was winding her arms around him. Very gently, he took her face between his two hands. Very gently, he drew her closer.

Suddenly he was kissing her and she was kissing him back. Fleetingly, she realised the youths had moved on, so no raucous hooting or whistles of derision troubled the couple kissing in the quiet alley. The only sounds were of muted chat and laughter drifting like smoke from the restaurant's open windows.

When the grumble of a diesel engine in low gear broke the spell, Zillah disengaged herself from Hal's embrace. She cleared her throat and grabbed the taxi's back-door handle, avoiding the driver's amused gaze.

'Taxi for Mrs Robinson?'

'Yes. Melbourne House, Henrietta Gardens, please.'

Silently, Hal followed her into the back seat, and pulled the heavy door shut. Zillah wriggled away so she was huddled in the far corner. Clunk! She fastened her seatbelt.

Hal secured his own belt and they sat in silence, listening to the happy sounds of reggae percolating from the speakers. Zillah sensed that he as well as she was concentrating hard on the passing street scenes, and not taking in anything. Neither seemed able to break the silence. Fortunately it was a short journey.

'Thank you very much. It's been lovely.' Zillah was out of the cab while Hal was still constructing a suitable comment that didn't seem too pushy. Was this a defining moment?

He pushed open his door and joined her on the pavement. 'Please, Zillah. Don't shut me out.'

His plea, so simple yet so heartfelt, melted any last negative feeling she had. Was that what she hoped he'd say? It wasn't in the least romantic. Yet could she — dared she — let her defences down?

Hal moved a little closer.

'Do you want to settle up, guv'nor?'

the driver called through his window.

'Pay the man,' she said, in a voice that didn't sound like her own. 'If you really want to come in, that is.'

★ ★ ★

She was very conscious of Hal's tallness, his broad shoulders and masculinity, as he followed her through the door. He waited until she'd secured it; and, as they faced one another, she smiled, seeing the anxious expression on his face.

'Am I such an ogre?' She walked towards the open sitting-room door. 'Maybe you shouldn't answer that.' She hesitated. 'Or maybe you should. I realise I must be very difficult to deal with.'

He was at her side in a beat, taking her in his arms. He held her to him, burying his face in her hair, whispering her name over and over again. She clung to him, hands roaming his shoulders, his back and his chest,

216

enjoying his taut muscles. She gave a little moan as he nuzzled her ear. Nothing mattered now. Only being in his arms and anticipating his lips upon hers. Their first kiss had shattered her resolve, sending her spinning into a vortex of indecision. She'd been grateful he'd kept his distance in the taxi. When he'd said nothing, she'd realised how frightened she was of his letting her go.

No. She didn't want to shut him out but she still wasn't sure of her emotions. They changed from day to day, surging like waves upon her beloved Cornish shores. The barriers she'd constructed on first encountering Hal had set up prickly moments; but now, on her own territory, she wanted him with an intensity that shocked her.

His mouth found hers. Their kiss deepened and sweetened, neither wanting it to end. When they finally moved apart, she stood there, gazing into his eyes, her fingers touching the pendant she wore so temptingly close to her cleavage. Hal traced his finger around the gemstone, traced its outline, his fingers feather-light on the delicate skin covering her collarbone. His touch sent tremors down her spine.

Being held in Hal's arms seemed so right. But after all the bickering and bantering, the carping and challenging, Zillah knew he wouldn't be content with cuddling. What if he thought of her as desperate? Needy? What could she say that wouldn't sound either dismissive or too seductive? She was so out of practice.

'You're trembling,' he said. 'Please don't be afraid, my sweet, lovely Zillah.'

His hands roamed over her shoulders and arms. Lulling her. If she wanted him to stop, she knew he would. But as his touch became more insistent, waves of pleasure melted her last shred of reticence.

'I want to make love to you, Zillah.' Hal's voice was low, his tone urgent. 'But you need to be sure, sweetheart.'

She caught hold of his hand, and led

him from the room and across the hallway.

'I'm sure,' she said.

*   *   *

Shocked into wakefulness by the clamour of the phone, Zillah's memory of the night before kicked in as she headed down the hallway. She hurried to answer, though it wouldn't be a business call on the flat's landline.

'Zillah, my dear. How are those fearful moggies behaving?'

How typical of her landlady to begin a conversation like this.

'All three are fine, Clarissa. They're eating well and there's nothing to report, really. How are you enjoying your stay?'

'Huh! I'm more than ready to come home. But my daughter-in-law's in agony — pulled a muscle in her back trying to be Serena Williams, silly girl. So I've decided to stay a few extra days so she can rest up. It's a case of sorting out meals for us all and keeping the laundry mountain from engulfing the household. Piece of cake, except I miss my peace and quiet. And my cats, of course.'

'Well, I'm not going anywhere but work for the next few days, so don't worry about the divas. I'm piling up your post in order of arrival. Your timer light's doing what it should. Oh, and I've found a flatmate for the next few months.' She'd suddenly remembered Zak.

'Nice gel, I hope?'

'She's a he. The cats approve.'

'Huh! Those little hussies are no judges of character.' Clarissa lowered her voice. 'I hope you didn't find this chap over the Internet. My daughter-in-law seems to get most things that way.'

'This chap's a singer and I met him through a business acquaintance. Zak is a very charming man.'

'Zak, eh? Might ask him in for a sherry one night. Now, I must go and walk this blessed dog. He's taken to following me around. Can't think why. Such absolute devotion's hard to handle after the divas' superciliousness. Goodbye now. Be good.'

Zillah felt her cheeks heat. What was that supposed to mean? Did her landlady think she and Zak were an item? But the connection was already cut, leaving no chance to discuss the rent surcharge. Well, whatever the amount, it would be shared by Zak. And Zillah's bank balance would look a whole lot healthier between now and September. After that, *Mrs Robinson* might actually be running at a healthy profit. *Dream on . . .*

The events of the night before came very firmly to mind when Zillah went into the kitchen to fix breakfast. Hal's note lay on the kitchen table.

Thank you for last night.

Zillah's cheeks burned as she recalled their long kiss outside the restaurant and the subsequent events. Whatever had possessed her? She must have squeezed her usual weekly units into a matter of hours. Then there had been that awful, strained cab ride, wondering whether to invite him in but convincing herself he'd think she was propositioning him. Zillah groaned out loud and sank onto a chair, putting her head in her hands.

How would she get their relationship back on a professional level? She didn't want to return to that frosty phase when they'd circled each other like prowling big cats. Equally, she didn't want him to think she was desperate for love. It was far too soon for that. Far too soon to contemplate another man sharing her life. Guilt consumed her. Relief flooded her because at least he hadn't hung around for breakfast. Had he forgotten they had an appointment that morning? This was what came of mixing business with pleasure, and it served her right.

★ ★ ★

When Zillah drove into the business park and headed for her building, she was surprised to see Hal already in the car park and sitting in his car. She was half an hour early on purpose, having been hoping to power up her computer and compose herself, ready for him to copy her spreadsheets before he examined the darned things. There was no point in her analysing them again. Not until he'd used his bean-counting skills to discover what she was doing wrong.

Hal got out of his car as Zillah locked her van. 'Hi,' he said. 'I was just catching up with the cricket score.'

'Good morning,' she said. 'You've beaten me to it.' Avoiding his eyes, she pulled a tissue from her pocket and rubbed at a non-existent mark on her windscreen.

'I didn't sleep too well,' he admitted. 'I, um, let myself out really early and went for a walk before I got into my car. Mickey made breakfast.' Hal paused. 'I told him I'd been to a party and crashed at a friend's house.'

Zillah felt her cheeks burn a second time. Mickey must have noticed them leave the bar together last night. Of course he did, because hadn't he given them a cheery wave and wished them a pleasant evening? This was awful. What had happened to her determination to keep a calm, impersonal demeanour? But Hal looked so gorgeous in that open-neck shirt the colour of sharp green apples. His legs seemed to go on forever in those well-cut dark jeans. She was finding it difficult to forget how wonderful it was last night, once more in the arms of a man tall enough to make her feel dainty. Once more to feel — oh, but it was better to curb such thoughts. The most important thing in her life was her livelihood, and she'd better remember that.

He unlocked the outer door and deactivated the alarm.

'I'll leave you to get sorted and come down at eleven, shall I?'

'Right. Yes. Fine, thanks.'

He headed upstairs without a backward glance. Had she really expected him to take her in his arms as soon as he'd closed the door on the outside world?

In her office, she called up the figures she needed to show him, and busied herself until she heard him bounding downstairs.

'All ready for you,' she said.

'Thanks.'

'You can check back to my first twelve months of trading. The current tax year's up-to-date so far, except for yesterday's function of course.'

'I'm impressed.' He sat down.

Immediately, Zillah bristled. 'I like things done properly,' she said. 'Even if I'm not a potential Businesswoman of the Year.'

She saw the hurt in his eyes.

'I never expected anything less of you, Zillah. And a lot of businesswomen would give every pair of Versace patent leather pumps in their wardrobe to have your ability. You can take it from me, not everyone's so professional.'

She didn't know whether to acknowledge his fashion know-how or to thank him for the vote of confidence. *What's wrong with me?* Tongue-tied, she stared at the wall.

'If it helps, I'll send these accounts to my email address. I don't want you to think you've got to hang around here when you've better things to do.'

Was he hoping she would stay around, and join him for lunch at The Golden Fleece to discuss the way forward? Was she hoping he'd suggest this? Would one of them be disappointed? Zillah wasn't sure whether the situation between had changed for better or worse.

'All right,' she said. 'I was only coming in this morning to try and figure out where I'm going wrong. I'm aware I need to attract more bookings, and I think you're probably right about my labour costs.'

'I can come up with an analysis based on the last three months and talk it through with you tomorrow morning. How's that?'

'Brilliant,' she said. 'Shall I make you some coffee before I get on?'

He shook his head. 'No, I'm fine, thank you. In fact, you can lock up when you're ready. I'm done here.'

She made no attempt to detain him.

★   ★   ★

'Mum, it's me. There's been a slight change of plan. Is it still all right if I drive over today?'

'Darling, of course it is. It'll be lovely to see you. We're not eating till at least half-past one, so you can sit in the garden with your father and drink homemade lemonade.'

'See you soon, then.'

Zillah replaced the phone. She checked her emails. No new enquiries. It seemed to her that, whatever Hal Christmas made of her bookkeeping, he couldn't produce new clients out of nowhere. *If only.* The good thing was, he seemed equally as keen as she was not to mention their night out. The whole thing had to have been alcohol-fuelled, and he was probably relieved she hadn't tried to hang around his neck. This way, they needn't see one another until the working week began; though, of course, she must spend time with him in the morning, having agreed.

She blocked out the image of the hurt in Hal's eyes when she'd spoken so briskly to him. Now she had almost twenty-four hours to get her act together — and that included convincing her stupid heart how low love and romance figured when it came to prioritising. Anyone with any common sense would tell her she was experiencing a knee-jerk attraction to Hal because she'd been deprived of romance in her life ever since losing her beloved Daniel. She still missed the hugs, the tender touches on her cheek; the surprise single red rose with her morning cup of coffee. Well, she'd just have to make do with memories.

★ ★ ★

The day became a sultry one, fortunately forecast by her mother, who produced a delicious cold lunch for the three of them. Zillah's father insisted on being left to clear the table and load the dishwasher.

'I'd love to go for a walk,' Zillah told her mum.

They followed a footpath leading from the guesthouse through nearby woods. Zillah lifted her face, thankful for the coolness beneath the thick canopy of trees.

'There's not much colour in your cheeks, darling,' said her mother.

'It's the heat, Mum.'

'And you're probably working too hard.'

Zillah sighed. 'I wish. It's very quiet at the moment, though there are a couple of big weddings coming up. I didn't want to talk shop at lunch.'

'But apart from the big weddings?'

'A trickle of bookings, but I live in hope.'

'And you're settling well in Bath. It's such a lovely city.'

'I love living in Bath.'

'This Zak sounds fun.'

'It's early days yet, but at least my monthly rent has reduced.'

'You know you only have to ask?'

'I know. That's why I didn't say anything in front of Dad.'

'I see.'

'Mum, it's fine, honestly it is. Abi is a brilliant assistant, and Hal Christmas is about to give me an analysis of my trading figures. I shall sort something out. Every event I cater offers the chance to attract new clients.'

'Of course — but don't forget what they say about all work and no play, Zillah.' Her mother glanced sideways at her. 'That's entirely your choice, my darling. At least you have a couple of men in your life, plus a loyal assistant.'

'Don't forget the cats! And Abi's

great at imaginative tweets and posting photos of luscious food on social media.'

'Yes, I do keep my eye open for those, but it's not my forte, is it?'

'You're not alone. There are still lots of people out there who rely on their local grapevine for information.'

They'd reached the lake. Zillah eyed the weeping willows, their fronds draping like crinolines over the water.

'So you have to do that thing you least like doing. Take a pile of business cards with you and call on places where you're not known. Some people still read adverts in the newsagent's window and supermarkets often have notice boards. The other thing you might try is to get the business written up in the local paper.'

'That's good advice, Mum, but I need to see what Hal comes up with tomorrow. That's the bottom line.'

Zillah had decided that, if he picked holes in her costings, she was prepared to take his advice. That was only sensible. But she needed to explore other avenues, as well as make sure that people like Mel the florist kept a stock of her cards. Women talked to their hairstylists and manicurists. They asked around if their daughter was getting married, often happier to go with the tried and trusted. It was her job to make sure *Mrs Robinson* was top of people's lists of the tried and trusted.

'So, what's he like, this Hal?'

'Very competent. Determined.'

'It's a strange combination, isn't it — an accountancy practice and an entertainments agency?'

'Yes.'

'I wonder what his star sign is.'

'I've no idea. I suppose he's quite ambitious. Better at planning than I ever knew how to be.'

Again her mother glanced sideways. 'Don't torture yourself, Zillah. I know it's a trite thing to say; but, well, Daniel wouldn't want you to spend the rest of your life alone.'

Zillah lifted her hair away from the

nape of her neck. 'I know, Mum. I — well, it's just too soon for me to think about dating again.'

'Ah.'

* * *

Driving back to Bath in the early evening, Zillah appreciated her vehicle's air-conditioning. As she drove through her gateway, she saw Zak's car parked in her landlady's space. She'd forgotten he might be back. She unlocked the garden gate to the accompaniment of a huge sigh. This was a new phase of her life — a flatmate to adjust to and a leaner, meaner approach towards her business.

Zak had, she was pleased to note, remembered to padlock the gate behind him. This was a quiet cul-de-sac, but house rules were there for a purpose. She heard the sound of a melodious male voice singing a song she recognised from an Andrew Lloyd Webber musical. She stopped, realising Zak was sitting on the bench, craftily positioned by Zillah to afford privacy. He must have been intent on his singing not to hear the gravel crunch beneath her feet.

But the performance stopped. 'What vision of loveliness doth approach?'

Zillah laughed. 'A rather crumpled one, unless of course you're talking to one of the cats. So, how was the big city?' She walked towards the voice.

'Cool, thank you. Not the weather, though. That was kind of muggy. But I caught up with lots of mates.' He stood up as she appeared. 'Excuse the shorts; it was mega hot in the car driving back. I really need a shower, but I didn't want to get in your way.'

'I usually shower in the mornings, but that was very thoughtful.'

'Mornings are the pits. I don't have to get up to go to work with the big guy tomorrow, but I need to talk seriously to him about prospects. So far, I've got one session doing voiceovers for a radio station in London. Fortunately that's next Friday, so it's another chance to badger my agent, poor guy.' He looked in no way repentant.

'A radio station? Good for you. Your friend Mr Christmas is thinking of approaching the local one on your behalf.'

'He is?' Zak brightened. 'That's interesting. But I hope you haven't been dallying with Hal in my absence.'

She felt her cheeks warm and wished they wouldn't keep doing that. 'Goodness, I'm still hot from the drive. I happened to bump into him in The Golden Fleece yesterday evening. We were talking business, and he mentioned trying to get you on the lunchtime magazine show.'

'The guy has to be bonkers. Talking business with a beautiful woman on a June evening after she's slaved all day at someone's wedding? Do I take it he's booked in at the pub while the builders bash his cottage about?'

'He is. At least, I think he said he was. And we're trying to help each other's businesses, you know. Why else would we spend time together?'

'You tell me. I might go and see him in a bit. I don't suppose you fancy coming with me for a quick drink? I'm sure he'd rather talk to you than me.'

'No,' said Zillah, noting the mischievous glint in Zak's eyes. 'It's nice of you to ask, but I thought I'd chill out with a book this evening. Make a sandwich, maybe. Not that I should. My mother fed me poached salmon, fresh asparagus and baby new potatoes. Dare I mention homemade raspberry trifle?'

'Sunday lunch with your folks? That's nice,' said Zak, rising. 'I kind of miss that.'

Before she could question him, he changed the subject.

'Here's Ruby come to find you.' He bent to pet the kitten. 'Hello, sweetcakes.' He straightened up again. 'Okeydoke, Zillah, I'll shower before I go rattle Mr Christmas's cage, and I won't forget to give him your love.'

He sprinted back to the house, ignoring her spluttered protests. A disgruntled Ruby mewed indignantly and sought refuge among the lettuces.

★　★　★

'You're not in this just for the love of it,' said Hal next morning in his office.

'I'm well aware of that,' said Zillah, bristling again. That was another thing he seemed to make happen. Her bristling. Had she ever done that before she met him?

He seemed back to the disdainful man she'd first encountered; and, although part of her was relieved to find he wanted to put their unexpected night together behind them, another part was slightly upset. All right, very upset. If only she hadn't welcomed him quite so enthusiastically. Despite efforts not to, she was still reeling from the gorgeousness of it. *Get a grip.*

'It's obvious your staffing level isn't right,' he said. 'I understand there are peaks and troughs within your bookings. That's inevitable. But it seems to me you're overcompensating your employees, rather than viewing them as part-time workers.'

'I'm not sure what you mean. It's only Abi who works part-time every week. I call upon Jake and the others as and when I need them. Their hourly rate reflects the size of the function.'

Hal pursed his lips. 'But Abi's rate fluctuates too. Why is that?'

'I think there's a difference between slicing cucumbers while listening to CDs, and working ten-hour shifts for Saturday weddings.'

'Work is work. You're an entrepreneur with a lot of acumen, but if you faff around, it won't help you or any of your staff. Do you want to be business-woman of the year? Then better start acting the part. You'll be better off. Believe me, Zillah.'

Stung, she thought of what her mother had said. She knew he was right. Oddly, she wondered how many shirts this man had. He always looked disturbingly fresh and crisp, while she

— Zillah felt sure — was becoming more and more like a limp lettuce. But she knew she should heed his advice if she wanted to survive.

'Abi needs her core hours increased. But the rate you pay her should be halfway between the minimum wage and the eye-watering amount she currently earns for an outside function. I note you don't charge yourself out at that rate.'

It was Zillah's turn to purse her lips. She knew her assistant would be up for some extra hours. But, without a calculator, Zillah wasn't sure how advantageous this new routine would prove for either of them. How was she supposed to keep Abi busy if there was a quiet patch, like this week, when her assistant wasn't in for today or tomorrow?

Hal must have read her mind. 'There must be stuff she can do upfront? You're bound to keep a certain amount in the freezer, for example?'

'I try not to,' snapped Zillah. 'People

expect and deserve freshly-cooked food.'

'Sure they do. But things like homemade stuffing, individual pastry cases perhaps — could they not be made in advance, freeing up you and Abi on a later occasion? Come on, you're the expert. Also,' he rumbled on like a bulldozer, 'you should be out and about drumming up business while your assistant stockpiles basic stuff you'll use in the near future.'

Had he been talking to her mum? Zillah puffed air through her lips. 'It sounds all right when you say it like that. In practice, I'm honestly not sure.'

'So, why not give it a trial run? Speak to Abi first and explain your aim. My guess is she'll be sympathetic. She enjoys working for you, and I'm sure she wants to keep doing so.' He consulted his notes and stared at the computer screen again.

What further glad tidings were hidden up his sleeve? Zillah wondered. Having to swallow medicine was never pleasant, but if he was good enough to give up his own time, she could hardly protest.

A series of short, sharp questions followed before Hal leaned back in his chair and made a steeple of his fingertips. 'It's not wonderful, Zillah. In fact, unless you can provide a cash injection — and soon — I'm afraid your next big event looks like being a cosy meeting with your bank manager.'

11

Hal shut his eyes and leaned his back against the door he'd just closed behind his visitor. Zillah was gorgeous. Right from that time their vehicles had almost mashed headlights when he was trying to locate the premises, he'd been attracted. So far, he'd done a great job in annoying her not once but twice. Probably a third time if you counted Saturday night.

He'd thought she wanted him as much as he wanted her, but maybe he'd been mistaken. He hated the idea of a one-night stand, and it irked him how Zillah seemed to have slotted what he'd hoped might be the beginning of a relationship into that category. Surely she wasn't that kind of woman? He didn't think so.

Now, with her barriers back in place, simply by giving her the facts and

242

telling the truth about her operating methods, he'd ruined her day. Week. Life. Did he care about that? Yes. After all those jerky encounters, those two occasions when they'd bumped into one another away from their offices — and now, most significant of all, having made love to her — he was smitten. Head over heels. He wanted to turn cartwheels. Wanted to rush out and buy a giant teddy bear, tuck a bouquet of red roses between the paws, and present him to her.

This wasn't his normal behaviour. Nor was this feeling convenient. He had builders to supervise while they worked on making his cottage lovable instead of merely habitable. He needed to keep his accountancy contacts sweet so they fed him jobs from the slightly more challenging clients with whom Hal excelled. Then there was the new business, the arm that he thought of as expressing his more zany side. Huh! So far he had two children's entertainers on his books, plus one golden oldie former radio DJ, adored by women of a certain age. The latter gentleman was a resident of Bath who hoped to enhance his CV by becoming sought after as an after-dinner speaker. That left Zak Silver.

Hal opened his eyes and groaned. Zak was the flagship client who knew how to hold an audience in the palm of his hand. He sang effortlessly, yet as if his life depended on pleasing the crowd kind enough to listen to him. Women worshipped him. Even Zillah had been prompted to offer him a flat-share, just like that.

When the singer had turned up at The Golden Fleece last night, Hal had been sitting in the beer garden, half-heartedly reading the Sunday colour supplements and sipping a lemonade shandy. Zak had ordered a plate of sandwiches and a large mineral water, and proceeded to remind Hal how much he needed work now he was staying around for a while.

'I did say I couldn't promise

anything,' Hal said, as soon as he could get a word in.

Zak had nodded. 'But you'll give it a whirl?'

'You're linked to my website, with a note saying you're available from now until September. Does that suit you?'

'I guess. Yeah, okay.'

'I'll contact the local radio station tomorrow and see if they express any interest in an interview.'

The singer had been pleased. But when he told Hal he'd offered to give him Zillah's love but she'd flipped her lid, a cold feeling spread through Hal's stomach.

'She was having a laugh,' Zak had said. 'But earlier, when I teased her, she made it quite plain the two of you were on a strictly business footing. So, I take it you won't mind if I ask her out to dinner some time? You know how attracted I am to her.'

Hal hadn't felt able to reiterate his original comments about keeping Zak's flat-share on a formal footing. It would have sounded like sour grapes. Zak was Zak, and if he asked Zillah out and she accepted, that was nothing to do with Hal. But, after his initial high, he felt desperately low. What an idiot he'd been to let Saturday's chance meeting progress as it did. He should have taken notice when he'd walked in on Zillah that time, and heard her telling Abi exactly how much she didn't fancy him. She was probably beating herself up over a white-wine-induced romantic liaison. Embarrassment would colour any further meetings.

He'd examined her accounts as promised. He was prepared to recommend her catering business as and when appropriate. But somehow he must convince himself this lady was not for him. Or else, he'd be putting himself on the line just as he had with Jessie. Sometimes he wished he could love 'em and leave 'em, as Zak did. But Hal, once he fell in love, found it difficult to fall out again.

If she really put her mind to it, Zillah found it surprisingly simple to avoid Hal. Yet, even with her office door firmly closed, it wasn't difficult to hear his footsteps on the stairs while she updated her website or dealt with enquiries. All essential preparations for her next function were complete, but Zillah, on reading the menu again and checking her store cupboard, discovered a couple of items running low. If she topped up today, Abi could begin preparing stuff for the freezer when she came in tomorrow. The answerphone could hold the fort while Zillah visited the supermarket. At the same time, she'd check for any new shops that might have popped up, including the kind of places aiming to dress the bride's mother. Jewellers, lingerie boutiques, even travel agents were all possibilities when it came to attracting more clients.

When Zillah snuck into her parking

space after her trip, it was early afternoon and there was no sign of Hal's car. She let herself into her office and cheered when she discovered two messages left for her to ring back with a quotation. She dealt with both of these immediately.

One prospect turned out to be someone considering options. The other was a request to cater a small engagement party. A delicious dinner for twelve people could, Zillah knew, pave the way to bigger business. If she pleased the starry-eyed couple on this occasion, maybe they'd ask her to quote for the wedding breakfast. There might be another engaged couple among the guests. She arranged to send suggestions via email.

Next on her list of things to do was a second meeting with Annie West. Zillah rang the number, waiting as the phone continued ringing until the answering service kicked in, then left a message, asking if it was convenient to call any afternoon that week.

She was still at her desk when she heard Hal's footsteps on the staircase. She hadn't heard him come in. Was it her imagination or was he hesitating outside her office before opening the outer door? When she heard the door close, she realised she'd been holding her breath. She couldn't resist getting up and going over to the window to watch his vehicle progress towards the slip road. How sad was that?

* * *

Abi was delighted by the offer of increased hours.

'Are you sure, Zillah? I know there's not much going on at the moment.'

'Hal Christmas has been kind enough to analyse my figures,' said Zillah. 'I have to admit what he says makes sense. Your core hours will increase, Abi. Your basic rate of pay is calculated so you're no worse off than when you were paid two separate rates. But of course there'll still be some flexibility regarding the days. Is that all right with you?'

'It certainly is. So, whatever hours I do, I'll earn the same rate whether I'm working at Planet Robinson or in someone else's kitchen or wherever?'

Zillah nodded. 'You got it. That'll apply to sitting here with me, chewing the fat. Or to peeling vegetables, piping cream into choux pastry cases — or juggling cool-boxes. You'll receive extra for working Sundays and Bank Holidays and of course, hours after midnight.' Zillah crossed her fingers under the table. She didn't want to lose Abi.

But her assistant was nodding. 'I see where he's coming from. There are things we can prepare up-front, rather than get here really early to do on the day of the function. It sounds to me this new scheme will suit both of us.'

'I hope so,' said Zillah. 'I'm also exploring the possibility of finding someone to decorate the celebration cake when we're asked to produce one — whether it's traditional, or a chocolate-and-Rich-Tea-biscuits cake like the one Prince William wanted on his wedding day.' She winked at Abi. 'It'd be good to find someone who could come in as and when necessary. Maybe someone who's trained, but finds it difficult to work normal hours because she has a young family? I could tweak my own schedule so I'm here to let her in during the evenings, maybe. If you know of anyone, I'd be interested.'

Abi sat up. 'One of my college lecturers is looking for something flexible. I still keep in touch with her. She's the one who provided a reference when I applied for my job with you.'

'I remember,' said Zillah. 'Well, get her to give me a call. You can say we might have something to interest her. Our specialist people are excellent, but their charges are quite hefty for a small outfit like ours. That's an area needing attention.'

'I'll text her. She might like to do that cake for the retirement party you mentioned, if you haven't already approached the other people.'

'You're a gem. No, that retirement cake is still one of my things to do. That's exactly the sort of input I need. Now, could you check my shopping list against the stores essentials and see if I've forgotten anything, please? Yesterday, I discovered the ground almonds stock was low.'

Abi's mouth became a round O of mock horror. 'How can the Marzipan Queen function without ground almonds?'

'I already bought some — couldn't risk disappointing you.'

★ ★ ★

A couple of days later, Zillah parked her car on the driveway of the beautiful house in which the West family lived. Having to stop for fuel, combined with Bath traffic ratcheted to snarling point by a heavy downpour, caused a later arrival than she intended. Already she felt damp and windblown from the garage forecourt when she grabbed her document case and jogged towards the front door. Although she dodged puddles while trying to prevent her hair from being whipped into a sticky mess against her lip-gloss, she still managed to splash the backs of her legs.

'Poor you.' Annie West's goddaughter let her in. 'Do you want to dive into the cloakroom?'

'Hi, Chloe. I'm obviously not good at hiding my feelings. I hate arriving looking a fright.' Zillah glanced down at her feet and groaned. 'I need to take my shoes off.' She stood first on one foot then the other.

'Follow me. It's horrid outside but you don't look a fright. That'd be impossible.' Chloe opened the door to a small but perfectly-formed cloakroom. 'You'll find everything you need in there. Annie's on the phone, so don't rush.'

Splashed legs, stained shoes and smudged eyeliner. *Way to go*. But the blip focused Zillah's mind on practicalities. Sometimes wedding planners forgot the distance between house and marquee when considering the possibility of the British weather playing the rain card on the big day. Offering a wedding planning service as well as catering for the reception would build on Hal's database idea. Why not think big?

Zillah made her way to the sitting-room. She hovered in the doorway until Mrs West noticed her and beckoned. Annie was using a walking frame today, resting one hand on it while she spoke on the phone.

She ended her call. 'Zillah, I'm sorry to be so rude. Please sit down. Has Chloe put the kettle on?'

'I expect so. She kindly offered me the cloakroom so I didn't walk in looking like Lorna Doone after hiking across the moors.'

Annie chuckled, sitting down carefully on a chair obviously designed for folk with mobility problems. She patted the arm. 'Can't decide whether to stay in my wheelchair for the wedding breakfast, or to have this fellow transported to the marquee. But that's the least of my problems.'

Zillah tilted her head to one side. 'Problems? Anything I can help with?'

Annie sighed. 'This is where I wish my daughter was back in the UK. I'm much more comfortable with horses and gardens than with wedding favours and temperamental singers.'

Zillah's antennae twitched. She leaned forward. 'Please don't think I'm interfering, but if I can take anything else off your list, I'm happy to do so.'

'I thought you were exclusively a catering service.'

'So did I.' Zillah lifted her chin. 'But more and more I'm finding myself having to sort out other things apart from food and drink. There are so many different items involved, and not everyone uses a wedding planner. In future, I shall be offering a checklist for my clients to use, to ensure they've thought of every tiny detail. If anything's been forgotten, I aim to fill the gap by suggesting specialist firms in the area.'

Annie blinked rapidly. 'Can you let me have one of these lists? And if I've missed something, will you do the necessary, please? I spend a lot of time working with a riding for the disabled charity, you see. My daughter's wedding is very important to me, but I do have a life as well!' Her grin was impish. 'Offspring sometimes forget that, I fancy.'

'I'll email you the list as soon as I make sure it's complete.' Zillah scribbled a reminder on her notepad. Such a document didn't actually exist yet, though it soon would. 'I also have a business contact, someone who provides entertainers, including a wedding singer.'

'Gracious, you don't mean karaoke for the evening do? How priceless. My two ancient aunties would adore that, given half a chance. But,' she mused, 'my husband would probably abandon ship.'

'I meant 'wedding singer' as in

someone who'd sing during the church service,' said Zillah. 'Though the tenor I'm thinking of is very versatile.'

'I might well consider him. My daughter's choice of singer seems to come with a lot of baggage. She asked if we could change the time of the ceremony, would you believe. So she could fit in a gig at another church beforehand. Our booking was confirmed before this other enquiry.'

'She's probably much in demand,' said Zillah soothingly. 'Singers are like everyone else in business. They aim to please their clients.'

'Well, she certainly won't please me by turning up late.'

Zillah deemed it wise to change the subject. 'Just let me know if you think I can help. I need to ask you questions about the marquee and the seating, if you can bear it.'

'I can bear it as long as I get my coffee — here comes Chloe right on cue. And she's remembered the Bath Oliver biscuits.'

Later, after she said goodbye to her client and drove back to the city, Zillah felt more cheerful. This was the kind of thing Hal Christmas had mentioned in his pep talk. Thinking outside the box, she thought wryly, though she hated the phrase. Would she run her idea by him?

To her horror, she imagined herself back in his arms, standing on the pavement, time suspended as she kissed him as if she never wanted to stop. It had been a *Titanic* moment — and look what it had led to! She wondered what possessed her to spend the evening with a man who clearly felt sorry for her, even though he'd heard her rude remark to Abi about not fancying him. *If he only knew.*

When she dropped into her office to check for messages, she decided she definitely wouldn't go to Hal with her fresh idea. She'd compile a list for Annie West, but first of all run it by her assistant. Abi went to so many weddings, she could probably do the job of wedding planner standing on her head.

Mr Christmas could sit on the back burner for the time being.

★ ★ ★

It still seemed strange to see Zak's silver Mini sitting in Zillah's landlady's paved parking space. She let herself into the apartment, wondering if her new flatmate was in tonight or out on the town. Zillah liked the idea of supper on a tray while watching a DVD. Except for the small matter of having forgotten to take something out of the freezer, which said a lot about her impeccable management skills.

Zak was sitting at the kitchen table. He jumped to his feet as she came through the door.

'Please stay where you are,' she said. 'This is your home now.'

He zoomed round the table to pull out a chair. 'You've been working. I haven't. Would you like a cup of tea? It's just brewed.'

'I should go for a jog,' she said. 'It's

stopped raining now, so I've no excuse.'

'So why don't I fix us a nice big salad for later?'

'You're on,' she said. 'I'll get changed, feed the divas, then get off.'

Zak was relieved to see her go. He needed a little more thinking time. Earlier, having spotted so many flat square shapes under all those old sheets and blankets in the third bedroom, he'd decided to investigate. What he'd discovered was still eating away at him. How could anyone, especially a savvy lady like Zillah, leave a horde like that in among a load of old paintings? The various landscapes and figure compositions weren't flamboyant enough for his liking. Maybe that was why Zillah had dumped the bundle of gold jewellery in with them. Nobody in their right mind would want to steal stuff like that. Did she even realise the jewellery was there? She'd told him she wasn't sure how many paintings her late husband had left. She needed someone to sort things out for her.

Zak had told Hal he'd made a fair bit of money when out in Las Vegas. This was true. He'd also squandered a large portion of it. Pretty women were often high-maintenance. His debts were at an all-time high. With several months to go before his next West End show run, he wasn't going to pay much off by doing wedding-singer gigs or hen nights. Zillah was a foxy lady, and she must be doing all right with that catering business of hers. It wouldn't hurt to borrow that bag of bling and take it to London when he went. He knew a guy who knew a guy. Once he'd established how much the stash was worth, he could tell Zillah.

He could picture her face as he gave her the figure. After deducting a suitable amount of commission to cover his trouble, of course. She would only expect such a thing, being an astute businesswoman.

★ ★ ★

Hal, hacking long grass with a scythe unearthed from the crumbling wreck his property's particulars had described as a garage, was wondering whether he really had done the right thing in moving to the country. Now that the builders were on the case, his cottage was at that difficult stage when people decided they must have been out of their minds to begin renovation. But it was good to be in the fresh air, though the grass was a little damp and he probably shouldn't be cutting it. All he wanted was access to the back door. There were plenty of tough briars and straggling branches to chop back, definitely the kind of task that should help to keep his mind off other matters — except, in the case of Mrs Robinson, it was failing dismally.

Too many times since the previous Saturday, Hal had analysed what had happened once that fantastic kiss sparked such a reaction. Prior to that, their meetings had been beset by freeze and thaw. He was pretty certain the desire centred on his side — but hadn't she fallen into his arms, their mouths meeting so beautifully, as if destined? Zillah had stirred his senses in every possible way. She wasn't just drop-dead gorgeous. She was intelligent, feisty and competent. Inwardly, he groaned. The description also fitted Jessie, his former partner. Perhaps he aimed too high when choosing a girlfriend.

But, he reminded himself, no way was Zillah his girlfriend, nor was she likely to be now. The interlude had taken place in the aftermath of a very pleasant dinner. And wine. She was probably kicking herself for getting too close and cosy with him when that crowd of youths surged past. That unlocking of her vulnerability triggered his protectiveness and his desire. Sadly, he suspected that that had been the end of a story barely begun. So why did he still hanker after a replay?

He threw down the rusty scythe and stretched his arms above his head. 'That's some sky,' he muttered.

Yellowish streaks against the rose, azure and gunmetal promised storms, but not until sunset strutted its stuff. He started slashing the last obstinate patch. Once he was finished, he could go inside and open his own back door for the first time. There was a great view from this garden. Much better than the view of townhouse roofs from Zillah's bench beneath the jasmine bush. He wished she could be standing next to him, listening to him talk about his plans.

'Stop it,' he warned himself. 'You don't stand even a ghost of a chance.' His next stroke of the scythe was vicious enough to threaten his balance. Knocked off course. That described his feelings. Plump raindrops were falling. It was time to drive to The Golden Fleece and see if the kindly landlady would knock up a bit of dinner for him.

12

Zillah was used to creating imaginative meals. She'd seen cake made in the form of a cricket pitch, a farmyard or a spaceship. Abi's former tutor had accepted the commission to decorate a retirement-theme cake, and Zillah was lost in admiration. The central figure stood upon silky green frosting, surrounded by reminders of his favourite pastimes. He wore tennis whites, and held a racquet in one hand but a tiny golf club in the other. A narrowboat was moored at one side of the cake. The husband's hobbies and long-awaited dream holiday with his wife were captured in sugar.

'She has real talent,' said Zillah, showing Abi when she arrived. 'The other people were good, but this work's quirky. There are little touches you don't notice at first, but when you do, you realise how clever they are. See how she's painted the name of the wife on the side of the ship?'

'I like the tiny terrier at his feet,' said Abi. 'I knew she'd do a great job. Cake icing's not my thing, as you know. Marzipan's much more easy. A bit like play-dough, really. So, what shall I start on now?'

'How about meringues? And maybe more meringues?'

Abi gave a mock salute. 'It seems to be working well, this upfront stuff?'

'I think so,' said Zillah. 'We're pacing ourselves better. Let's see how we feel tomorrow. Hopefully, there won't be quite so much pressure on us in the morning.'

Piles of goodies grew as the two worked together on the party food. This function venue was a golf club in Gloucestershire. Zillah knew it well. A husband-and-wife team made an excellent job of running the bar and basic menu, but didn't feel inclined to take on big catering jobs. She got on well with the couple and knew this booking was doubtless down to them. It would be diplomatic to put some money into the collecting box of their favourite charity. A bottle of wine or bunch of flowers would be like taking strawberries and cream to Wimbledon. She must also ask if she could pin one of her own cards — plus a Hal Christmas Agency one — on the club's notice board. Zillah was trying hard to make the most of every possible opportunity.

On the practical side, the unsuspecting golf addict whose retirement was being celebrated would be out on the course from eleven o'clock onwards, playing with his regulars. Zillah would deliver the food and arrange it on the tables in the function room. His wife would arrive well before the golfers were due back at the nineteenth hole, bringing suitable clothes for her husband to change into for his surprise party.

★   ★   ★

Hal didn't relish another weekend in the pub. His office work was pretty much up-to-date, so he planned to spend Saturday redecorating his bedroom now that the builders had re-plastered where necessary. He'd bought far too much paint for his new office, so using it in this way made for a neat solution. The rewiring wasn't finished yet, so he drove into Bath on Saturday morning to buy a small camping stove and items for a picnic.

Heading out of the city again, he struck the steering wheel with the palm of his hand. 'Damnation,' he said. 'What an idiot.' He'd forgotten to load the paint and brushes in his car boot the night before. He'd been working on a client's accounts, trying to complete them to leave the weekend free for the cottage. If he was honest, he hadn't wanted to risk bumping into Zillah that morning. But it was too late to worry about that. He scolded himself for being so paranoid.

He turned off for the business park,

crawling in low gear along the road leading to his premises. One never knew who might be travelling in the other direction. Sure enough, the silver van was parked near the front door. That meant Mrs Robinson would be loading up and on the road before long. He pushed open the front door, whistling a song he'd heard Zak singing once or twice. It was all about unrequited love. Hal stopped whistling, coughed guiltily, scooped up his post and took the stairs two at a time.

Zillah, checking her emails, heard his feet pounding towards the top floor and frowned as her heartbeat upped its rate. Couldn't the wretched man keep away from the place? Though, to be fair, life couldn't be much fun for him just now, lodging at the pub while being effectively barred from living in his cottage. Still, that was his choice. He must have realised how much TLC was required when he bought the property.

She was still at her desk when she heard Hal descend from the upper regions, this time much more slowly. There was a muffled thud and an exclamation. It seemed churlish not to check on him. Zillah opened her door as he arrived at the bottom of the stairs and plonked two large drums of paint on the floor. His bundle of brushes, cleaned and secured in a big elastic band, lay on one of the stair-treads. The sight of denim jeans clinging to a trim masculine rear, their owner stretching up to recover the dropped items, greeted Zillah.

She averted her gaze. But not before noticing the lightly-tanned skin exposed between the edges of T-shirt and jeans waistband.

'Everything all right?' She hovered in her doorway.

'Everything's fine, thanks. Hope I didn't disturb you?' He tucked his brushes under one arm and picked up the paint cans.

Zillah couldn't avert her eyes any longer. Not without seeming extremely rude. But when her gaze met his, there it was again: that treacherous thump-bump-bump of her heart.

'I was just checking in case someone had fallen downstairs,' she said without conviction.

'I'm off to do some decorating.' He swallowed hard, not moving.

'I'm about to deliver food for a retirement party.' She didn't move either.

Abi, pink-cheeked and cheerful, poked her head round the kitchen door. 'I've finished, now, Zillah. Oh, hi there, Hal. Sorry — um, didn't mean to interrupt.'

Zillah was standing there, barefoot, having left her work clogs inside the kitchen door. Fighting a powerful urge to go up to Hal and kiss him, she was so unwound with longing that she darted towards Abi just as he moved forward. They collided. The bundle of paintbrushes fell from under Hal's arm. Again.

Abi ducked back into the kitchen.

Zillah followed her inside and closed the door.

Abi spoke rather too loudly for her employer's liking.

'Can't you two clowns realise how attracted you are to each other? I'm sorry if I sound blunt, but someone has to say it.'

★ ★ ★

Zillah glided as if on rollerblades between golf club kitchen and function room, delivering dishes and platters to the buffet table. She'd decided to work this one alone. Once everything was arranged, she could leave and return later for her equipment.

'It all looks gorgeous, Zillah.' Amy, the club stewardess appeared in the doorway. 'What a fabulous cake!'

'Thank you, though the decoration's not down to me.'

'These people want to be left alone, I gather. All very informal, they said.'

'Yes, it's an easy gig. It's an easy cake to cut, too. Soft sponge, butter cream and icing.'

272

'Shame to spoil it, I reckon. It's a work of art.'

'They'll probably take loads of photos. Hopefully the cake will turn up on social media, if I know my assistant. I'll come back at around six to clear the debris, if that's all right?'

'Perfect. Are you working anywhere else today?'

'Sadly, no.' Zillah felt in her pocket. 'That reminds me. I wonder if you'd let me put one of my cards on your notice board.' She hesitated, holding up Hal's card too. 'This entertainments agency and my firm are promoting each other's services.'

'No problem.' Amy glanced at the cards. 'Hal Christmas Agency — now there's a name you wouldn't forget in a hurry.'

Zillah drained the glass of lime and soda water she'd been sipping on and off. She didn't want to talk about Hal. Didn't want to remember the words he'd whispered in her ear. Didn't want to imagine his arms holding her.

Keeping things on a strictly business level was not as straightforward as she'd hoped it would be.

On the way to her van, Zillah was surprised to hear someone call her name. She stopped and turned round to find she was looking at a man who'd purchased several of her late husband's paintings over the years before Daniel's death.

'It really is you! How strange our paths should cross like this, Zillah.' He held out his hand, beaming.

'Lionel! What are you doing in this part of the world?'

'We moved from London not long after we got your letter, telling us about Daniel.' He hugged her briefly. 'I'm so sorry, Zillah. It must have been devastating for you. I don't know what to say, really.'

'You wrote me a beautiful letter.'

'I meant every word. Apart from being a lovely man, he was such a talent. And deserved more recognition than he received, in my humble opinion.'

'Ah, but he was happy that way. Daniel didn't want the big time — all the glitzy parties. He liked nothing better than a pint in the local and a chat with the fishermen.'

'I gathered that when my wife and I came to Cornwall that time. I got up at sunrise and walked down to the quayside with him to watch him sketching. It was a privilege. He became almost part of the landscape. Something I'll never forget, Daniel's hands bringing the scene to life. The light. It was magical.'

The two stood in silence. Zillah could hear the seagulls. See Dan's hands moving swiftly, like the currents the fishermen treated with such respect. She had to swallow hard. 'How many of his paintings do you have, Lionel? About five?'

'You have a good memory. But I'd like more. I don't suppose you've changed your mind about selling some of his work? Forgive me if I'm speaking out of turn.'

She shook her head. 'That's all right. But I need to sort through the canvases. Somehow I can't bring myself to do so yet.'

'Understandable,' said Lionel. He glanced down at her crisp uniform. 'But anything by Daniel Robinson would be much sought after. If you needed to raise funds, I mean.' He glanced at his watch. 'I'm sorry, but I have to meet my caddy. I'm still a new boy here. May I take your phone number? What exactly are you doing these days?'

Zillah pulled out a *Mrs Robinson* card. 'I run my own gourmet catering business. This club's just on the borders of my catchment area. I live in Bath now.'

Lionel nodded. 'I'll give your card to She Who Must Be Obeyed. If number-one daughter decides to marry from home, we'll certainly bear your services in mind.' He squeezed her elbow. 'Take care. And, should you ever decide to sell any paintings, please do email me, my dear.'

'I shall. It's great to see you again, Lionel. Please give my best regards to your wife.'

Zillah was deep in thought as she drove back to Bath. She had to force herself not to drive on autopilot, especially on the more challenging cross-country roads. Meeting Lionel had been a confrontation with her past. Longing — for Cornwall, for her former life, and especially the love she had shared with her late husband — engulfed her. She raised a hand and angrily brushed away a tear trickling down one cheek. Why did such a lovely man have to be taken from her when he had so much more to give? There had been a haunting quality to his work. That's why the Cornish fishermen thought so much of him. He captured not only the sunlight on the water and the storm clouds dominating the sky. Within those splashes of gold and silver, violet and apricot, he could also depict dedication, guts, and the vulnerability and vigour of the crews.

But Daniel was gone. She was on her own and, in spite of her efforts to heed Hal's advice, Zillah knew her financial situation was as fragile as one of those fishing boats pitted against the elements. Maybe it was time to heed Lionel's advice and take note of her assets. A cash injection into her business bank account would help matters. She knew that. Hal Christmas knew it too. But selling those precious pictures was going to be like having Daniel wrenched away from her all over again.

'And if I sell that jewellery,' she murmured to herself, 'it'll be yet another link broken.'

Or maybe she should cut and run. But where to? And what would she do? The thought of another move made her feel wretched. And a little voice deep inside her told her not to take the coward's way out.

★ ★ ★

That wretched song was bugging Hal again. It was playing in his head as he slapped country primrose emulsion on his bedroom ceiling. It danced into his head after he brewed tea downstairs in a kitchen resembling a war zone. That wasn't all down to the builders either. Hal still had stuff bursting from the bulging black plastic bags he constantly shifted from room to room. A bit like his life at the moment, though at least his finances were healthy. There were even a few bookings slowly creeping in via the entertainments agency website.

Hal much preferred order to chaos. He was still standing on the stepladder when he drained his mug of tea and turned to plonk it down on the draining board. Too late, he realised the latter equipment was not yet fitted.

★　★　★

Zillah heard a phone ringing as she let herself into her flat. It sounded like Zak's zany ringtone, but he was in

279

London. How come? In the kitchen she soon realised he'd gone off without his mobile. How irritating for him. She hesitated, wondering whether to answer the call and decided that, if it happened to be Zak calling his own number, at least she could reassure him his phone was safe and not stolen.

'Hello,' she said cautiously. No way was she going to give either Zak's name or her own.

Silence was followed by a voice that sounded as if the owner was straining it through gritted teeth. 'Is Zak Silver available, please?'

Zillah didn't recognise the gruff tones. 'I'm sorry. He appears to have left his phone behind.'

'Zillah? Is that you?'

She frowned. 'Yes. Who is this?'

'It's me. Hal. I've done something very stupid, and I was hoping Zak could get me out of a jam. But don't worry. I can ring for a taxi.'

'You don't sound your usual self. Are you sure you can cope?'

He grunted. 'I lost my balance on the stepladder, and somehow I've damaged my ankle in the fall. It's not broken, I fancy, but it's probably a bad sprain.'

'What rotten luck.' She thought for a moment. He obviously had no one else to call upon if he was ringing Zak. She made up her mind. 'I'll come and collect you. I guess the ED is the right place for you.'

'The what?'

'I mean the Emergency Department at the Royal United Hospital. How do I find you?'

She listened carefully. It sounded as if Hal's ankle hurt like hell. Her car keys were still in her hand.

Zillah drove down the London Road. She wasn't bad at following directions, and preferred not to use a satellite system for navigating the area. Hal sounded in bad shape. She hoped she didn't take any wrong turnings.

Zak's phone, which she'd brought along in case Hal rang again, began to play the opening chords of *Ride of the*

Valkyries again the moment she turned off the main road. Zillah ignored it. Whoever it was this time would have to wait. She wondered whether Hal would be able to walk to her van from wherever he was waiting.

But, as she steered between banks of lacy cow parsley and hedgerows veiled by pink dog roses, she saw a figure slumped at the roadside. He was waving at her. Thump, thump went her heart. Tears filled her eyes. She was being ridiculous. If Hal Christmas could walk as far as his gate, he was obviously not at death's door. Maybe she should have left him to ring for a cab after all. Put him right out of her mind. He was waving frantically now. Why would he do that? Did he think she couldn't see him? He lurched backwards and toppled against the hedge as she bumped through the gateway and onto the sloping driveway.

Zillah jumped from her van and strode back to where Hal sat dejectedly on a tree stump.

'What was all that about?' She stood over him, hands on hips.

'I was trying to stop you from driving in. Trying to be helpful. Vision's dreadful, coming out of my gateway. There's a farm track leading back to the main road if you continue the way you were coming.'

'Fascinating,' she said coldly. Did he think she wasn't capable of turning her van on a fifty-pence piece? 'Let's get you to the hospital.' She saw no sign of an overnight bag. 'Do you have everything you need?'

He was still sitting on the ground. 'I don't know. Credit Card. Money. Phone. Do I need anything else?' He struggled to get up.

She held out both her hands. 'I meant basic stuff in case they keep you overnight.'

'Keep me in? He sounded alarmed. 'Why would they do that? It's only a ricked ankle. I suffered much worse in my rugby-playing days.'

She almost retorted that he'd been a

lot younger then. 'Well, all right, if you're sure. You can obviously bear your own weight.'

He grimaced as he struggled to his feet. 'It feels like I've got a ball and chain on my right foot. Thanks, Zillah.'

She waited while he manoeuvred himself into the passenger seat, managing to bang his head on the half-open door, an action he followed by sitting on Zak's phone.

'Some days are just not meant to go right,' he said.

Zillah was seized with an uncontrollable urge to giggle.

'I'm glad you find it so funny,' he snapped.

They stayed silent on the way to the hospital. She had to drop him off at the Emergency Department entrance, and find someone to help her dump him in a wheelchair. Once she'd squeezed into a parking space miraculously available, and returned to find Hal, a triage nurse confirmed that the patient would live. His ankle was swollen but not broken.

It would probably be about two hours before he could see a doctor. Hearing this, Hal growled from his wheelchair. Zillah elbowed him in the ribs, and immediately felt guilty for adding to his pain.

'I think you'll need that ankle strapped for support,' said the nurse. 'I'm ordering an X-ray just to confirm my opinion. If you wait in the blue seating area, you'll be called soon.' She turned to Zillah. 'There's a café near the main entrance, Mrs Christmas. You can bring something back for your husband. He won't be undergoing an anaesthetic.' She smiled reassuringly.

'He's not — ' Zillah thought better of it. The nurse must have noticed her wedding ring. 'Thank you,' she said.

She noticed how Hal was looking up at the nurse then turning back to her. Two women talking over his head must be an alien experience for a man of his height and personality. Zillah wondered if he expected her to wait with him. Probably not, but she couldn't bear to think of abandoning him.

She pushed the patient towards the blue seating area, parking the chair neatly at the end of the front row and even remembering to apply the brake. 'Hal, I need to go outside and check out a call to Zak's mobile. I couldn't pick up while I was driving, and it might be him, trying to establish who has his phone.'

'Okay. But I can't expect you to hang around here all day. You've got things to do. I can ring for a taxi when they let me go.'

'And where do you propose telling the taxi to take you?' She knew he'd got down the stairs on his behind and somehow made his way by hopping and shuffling down to the gate. Mickey and his wife were brilliant, but it was hardly fair to expect them to care for Hal in his current state. She'd checked out the guest rooms in their pub and knew none were on the ground floor.

Hal looked so crestfallen that Zillah, for all her crisp manner, wanted to put her arms around him and smooth away that little-boy lock of hair falling over one eye. She looked at her watch. 'I'm not in any rush. I'll go and check that phone, then fetch us something to eat and drink. It'll help pass the time and keep your blood sugar level from plummeting.'

She reached for a magazine and plonked it in his lap. 'It's not the *Financial Times* but you might enjoy reading about celebrity life for a change.' Seeing the horrified expression on his face, she suppressed a chuckle. 'I promise not to be long.'

13

Was his voice a tad too exuberant? For some reason, returning the call to Zak's mobile phone, Zillah thought the singer sounded as if he'd been up to something he shouldn't. If she was being honest, he sounded almost ingratiating. Anyway, it was a strange kind of hunch to have, especially considering the brief time she'd known the man.

'I really am sorry to be such a pest, Zillah. Serves me right for leaving in so much of a hurry,' he said. 'Maybe I need a minder? Would you fancy the job?'

'Excuse me? I've got enough on my hands, sorting out your friend.'

'Sorry — say again?'

'Your friend Mr Christmas dived off a stepladder at lunchtime. I'm phoning from the hospital.'

'Wow. Poor guy. Will he live?'

'I think so, but he's wrenched his ankle quite badly. Hurt his pride. He'll certainly be out of action for a while. When is it you come back to Bath?'

'The good news is, my agent's got me a couple of auditions this coming week. Why do you ask? Missing me already?' This was more the Zak she knew.

'I'll survive,' she said. 'But I'm wondering where Hal's going to go after they've done all the things they have to do. Does he have any friends in the area, do you know?'

'Not to my knowledge,' said Zak. 'Probably hasn't had time to make any yet. How come you got involved?'

'He rang your mobile just as I walked into my kitchen.'

'Knowing Hal's opinion of me, I guess that means he was pretty desperate. So you picked up the call?'

'Yep. I collected him from his cottage. Does he have a phobia about women drivers, by the way?'

Zak laughed. 'I wouldn't be surprised.'

'More importantly, do you have any suggestions as to what happens next?'

'Can't the guy go back to The Golden Fleece?'

'I don't think so. Those stairs are picturesque but not user-friendly. He'd be stuck in his room and Mickey and his staff would have to trail up and down with meals and drinks. No, I think there's only one thing for it.'

'Don't tell me you've decided to put him in my bed.' Zak's merriment bubbled through the phone.

'Well, yes, as a matter of fact I have, unless you strongly object. But I can't see anything remotely humorous about it.'

'I can hardly object, seeing as he let me stay at his cottage till you rescued me. If you two haven't murdered each other by the time I return, I guess I can always take over Hal's room at the pub.'

★ ★ ★

290

When the call ended, Zak, sitting on his mate's balcony in Clapham, stared sightlessly into space. He thought his acting skills had helped him act naturally with Zillah — but, oh, what a muppet he'd been to leave his mobile phone in her flat! He told himself to remain calm.

If she discovered the bundle of gold was missing, there had to be several suspects. Like removal men and the tradesmen she mentioned who'd sorted out the boiler. He just needed to keep his cool. After all, he was doing her a favour. Without his intervention, those canvases would probably sit there for the next few years. He could sort it. Given time. He felt hot and cold with relief as he realised that the buyer of gold he planned to visit didn't have his mobile phone number.

With a bit of luck, Zillah would have her work cut out keeping an eye on Hal, plus those cute cats, as well as running her business. Zak had enough buoyancy to float the *Titanic*. Everything would be fine. He just needed a little more time. Meanwhile, he didn't fancy Hal's chances when it came to his temporary nurse's bedside manner. Maybe she'd be so fed up with Hal's abrasive comments, she'd be ready to give Zak a doubly warm welcome when he returned with the kind of news he reckoned on giving her. Zillah might be easy on the eye, but he reckoned it would take a very brave man to criticise her driving — or her cooking, for that matter.

* * *

Zillah walked back inside, bought sandwiches and coffee and returned to the blue seating area to find Hal staring into space, the magazine she'd offered him, abandoned on a chair.

'Thank you, but I'm not sure I can eat anything just now,' he said. 'Maybe later.'

She didn't argue but handed him a bottle of water.

'Perfect. Thanks. So did you speak to Zak?' He unscrewed the bottle top.

'He says he's very sorry to hear about your accident and he won't be back for a few days so you're welcome to use his room. It's obvious you need to be on the ground floor so you can get to the bathroom and so on.' The words poured out in a rush.

Hal groaned and swigged water from the bottle. 'I've been sitting here, trying to come up with a solution. I know Mickey's pub is off-limits. They've got enough to do without waiting on me. But I can't, I just can't, intrude on you like this, Zillah.'

'Do you have any better ideas?' She sat down beside him and unscrewed the top of her own water bottle.

'None. I haven't a clue what I can do. You could always parcel me up and send me to my parents in Norfolk, I suppose.'

'I'll take that as a yes, then? You'll

accept Zak's and my suggestion, I mean?'

'I still think it's monstrously unfair and highly embarrassing, but if you're prepared to put up with me, I guess I have no other option.'

'Thanks for the vote of confidence. I imagine I could find a nursing home to take you temporarily,' she teased. 'I realise I wouldn't be your number-one choice for a carer.'

Her throat constricted as her eyes met Hal's and she saw the vulnerability reflected in them. She turned away, for fear he might detect the longing in hers. It would be so easy to get up and put her arms around him. She pushed the thought from her. To be brushed away would be chastening and whatever either of them felt about the other, they needed to keep their relationship strictly businesslike.

The pair sat in silence, sipping their drinks, until Hal's name was called and Zillah pushed him to keep his date in the X-ray suite.

'Do you feel more comfortable now?' Zillah was negotiating the city traffic.

'Yes, fortunately,' said Hal. 'I could still kick myself for being so careless, though.'

'Better not try that,' she said, pulling away from the traffic lights. 'You might do the other ankle in.'

'If my mobile hadn't bleeped just as I was trying to put down my mug, I don't think I'd have stepped back into thin air,' he said gloomily.

'At least when you fell, you could reach it to make a call,' said Zillah.

'Hmm. Suppose so. It wasn't even anything important. Just my phone provider offering an upgrade.'

What was important, thought Zillah, was that Hal seemed to have nobody near at hand except Zak — and now herself. At least, if the situation had been reversed, she would have had Abi close by; and, even if they lived thirty miles away, her mum and dad.

'Zillah,' said Hal. 'We must talk practicalities. I know I have to rest, but I can't expect you to run round after me. Could I ask you to buy some ready meals or something? I can't have you cooking for me on top of everything else.'

'You're treading on dangerous ground here, Mr Christmas.'

He glanced at her profile and grinned. 'I'd better rephrase what I said, then. How about, you spend enough time cooking marvellous meals for other people without adding me to the list?'

'You'll be doing me a favour by helping eat up some food. Zak bought stuff he can't possibly use now, and I always keep the freezer stocked with single portions.' *Whoops! That sounded sad. True, though.*

'Well, somehow I'll find a way of repaying your kindness.'

'You already have, by analysing my figures and advising me how to streamline my business.' She could have added, 'Before it's too late', but didn't.

They were driving over Pulteney Bridge. Tourists, many in colourful shorts and T-shirts, peered into shop windows and took photographs. Zillah remembered the evening she and Hal had met by chance in her favourite café and spent time together. Her stomach lurched as her brain flipped back to the pizza supper when, ever so slightly tipsy, they'd kissed outside the restaurant. How could she have done that? And how could she now be driving this enigmatic man back to her flat, treating him so very differently from the way she had when both of them ached to forget their lonely lifestyles? She couldn't prevent a smile when it occurred to her that the neighbours might wonder if she was taking in paying guests while Clarissa was away. Or worse.

'So, what's so funny this time?'

Without thinking, she reached out a hand and patted his. 'I was just thinking how intrigued the neighbours might be if they see a second male person arriving with me and disappearing inside my flat.'

Hal shifted in his seat. 'I hadn't thought of that. Maybe you should put up a little notice saying 'Waifs and Strays Welcome'?'

Zillah clicked on the left-hand indicator. 'Maybe, but only as long as I put up a 'No Vacancies' notice at the same time. One walking-wounded male plus three cats, albeit temporarily, are quite enough for me, thanks.'

Hal, aided by crutches, got himself through the garden gate and inside. Zillah pulled out a chair so he could sit at the kitchen table.

'I'm going to make a pot of tea, and toast and Marmite,' she announced. 'Would you like me to switch on the television?'

'Oh, Lord, this is uncomfortable for you, Zillah. You need your own space. I presume Zak was out far more than he was in. I'll be hanging around like an unpleasant smell.'

He was glowering so much that

Zillah laughed again. 'Come on, Hal — make the best of it. You'll probably only need to rest up for a matter of days. What's that set against a lifetime? Now, do you want toast, or cheese and biscuits? You should eat something to keep you going.'

'Toast and Marmite sounds great.'

'Classic comfort food,' she called over her shoulder as she filled the kettle.

'I'm sorry you wasted money on those sandwiches.'

'Ah, but that young couple sharing a milkshake were very grateful. We'll have something more substantial this evening, don't worry — though probably not before eight, I'm afraid. I have to collect my equipment from the golf club.'

'Was that a wedding buffet?'

'No, a retirement party with loads of nice nibbles, and a heavenly cake made by Abi and decorated by her old lecturer. She did a fantastic job at a very reasonable cost. You see, I'm putting some of your suggestions into practice already.'

He was concentrating on a small watercolour on the opposite wall. 'Um, good,' he said absent-mindedly. 'Just admiring your farmyard picture. Those hens are real characters.'

'Priceless, aren't they? You'll find lots of pictures in this flat.'

'I imagine this one's by a favourite artist of yours? I don't know a great deal about art, but I do know what I like. This picture makes me feel I could reach out and stroke those feathers.'

The grill popped into life and Zillah slid four slices of bread beneath it. 'I'll stand here,' she said. 'I have an awful habit of leaving toast to brown, then walking away and incinerating it.'

He nodded. 'We all have our faults.'

She regarded him, head on one side. 'Like forgetting where we're standing?'

'Touché. My concentration hasn't been brilliant lately.' He bit his lip.

Zillah poured scalding water into a chubby daisy-splattered teapot. It struck her each of them was skilful at avoiding certain topics. Hal was probably still brooding over his broken relationship. Would he really want to hear about the sturdy French hens, captured forever by her late husband's skilful fingers?

On their honeymoon, she and Daniel had stopped at a farmhouse bed-and-breakfast on first arriving in Brittany. Friends had teased them about exchanging Cornwall for its French equivalent. But Zillah would have honeymooned in their back garden as long as she could be with Daniel.

She flipped the bread slices over. 'This won't be long. I'll just get some spread from the fridge, so you'd better pray I don't fall over my feet and leave the toast to burn while you struggle in vain to rescue it.'

'You're a sadistic woman, Mrs Robinson. All of a sudden I'm starving.'

Hal was absolutely gorgeous when he smiled. He had even white teeth, and his eyelashes and eyebrows were much darker than his hair. There was also the fact that he liked Marmite. It would be good if they could become friends while sharing the same roof. After all, they were old enough and big enough to put past embarrassments behind them and face the future. It seemed to her they could each use a friend. If only she could stop herself noticing how darned attractive he was. If only she could stop remembering the touch of his lips on hers.

* * *

Hal thought Zillah seemed unusually serene as she showed him where he'd be sleeping. After she left him in the sitting-room with the radio on and set off for the golf club to complete her chores, Hal straight away rang The Golden Fleece.

'Mickey? Hal Christmas here. I'm afraid I've done my ankle in and I'm currently using crutches. Zillah, bless her, drove me to the hospital, and now

I'm at her place, having to stay in Zak Silver's room. Obviously I'll continue paying you for my accommodation, but if Zak arrives unexpectedly, he'll have to take it over, given that I'm stuck on the ground floor for the time being.'

Hal listened and grinned. 'Did you say you'd need to lock up your wife and your barmaid? I like your style, Mickey. Zak's heart is in the right place, though. I think.'

He listened and chuckled again. 'Look mate, I know this is an awful cheek on a Saturday evening but is there any way you could get two suppers and a bottle of that great Chablis along to Zillah's place?'

Mickey's chuckle rumbled into the phone. 'Don't tell me the lady's gone off cooking?'

'As she's taken pity on me, I want to surprise her. Save her some work. Tell me if you're too busy and I'll organise a takeaway.'

'Zillah enjoys a glass of white wine after a hard day,' said Mickey. 'We'll sort it, you lucky devil, you. My wife's beside me and she's nodding. We'll get Jake to deliver a bottle, plus two portions of salmon in filo pastry with runner beans and new potatoes. He knows where Zillah lives.'

'Could you put the lot on my account, please? Oh, and a dessert would be great too. Cheers, Mickey.' Hal ignored a cheeky comment from the landlord and ended the call, feeling relieved. At least, even if he was forced to make like an invalid for a while, he could provide a treat for Zillah that evening. Mickey's wife was going to pack his toiletries and towels, plus a few other necessary items. What a nuisance he was turning out to be — but at least he wouldn't have to ask Zillah to drive him to the cottage to collect clothing. The thought of her having to riffle through his socks and boxers was disconcerting, to say the least.

★   ★   ★

Hal was watching the evening news when he heard Zillah come back.

'It's me. As soon as I've changed, I'll start supper.' She put her head round the sitting-room door.

'I have a confession to make. I hope you don't mind but I've ordered in some food.'

She looked taken aback. 'Right. Yes, that's great. Thank you. What are we having?'

'It's a surprise.'

'I'm afraid there isn't any wine. I think Zak and I finished the last bottle the night before he left.'

'No problem,' said Hal.

'Did you remember to explain about the garden entrance? If the delivery person knocks at the front door, I probably won't hear the bell from here.'

'It's all sorted. Trust me.'

Zillah threw him an evening newspaper and disappeared.

'Thanks,' he called, opening it at the sports section. But no sooner had he finished an article about Bath's cricket

305

team than she was back. She'd changed into a scoop-neck black top, with pink cotton cut-offs accentuating her long, shapely legs. The garments were easy on the eye, but not good for his state of mind.

'I'll pop along to the off-licence,' she said. 'A glass of wine would be relaxing after today's events.'

Before Hal could reply, his mobile phone rang. 'Don't go, Zillah, please,' he said, answering it.

He watched her hover, a puzzled expression on her face.

'Okay, Jake,' he said. 'I'll ask Zillah to open the side gate so you can bring it in. Thanks a lot, mate.'

Zillah nodded her understanding and set off.

Hal smiled to himself. Hopefully she'd be far more appreciative of The Golden Fleece's menu than the normal sort of takeaway fare. Nor would she be opening her purse, as Mickey's instructions were to put everything on Hal's bill.

He heard her call, 'Thanks again, Jake. Sure there's nothing else in your car? No odd sock? Good. I'll see you soon.'

Shortly after came the sound of the back door being closed. It was that kind of door. Not long after that, Zillah appeared, carrying a small tray on which stood two large glasses of white wine. She was smiling.

'That was a very cunning manoeuvre, Mr Christmas.' She handed him a glass. 'I'm impressed. What's more, you must have impressed Mickey. Or his wife,' she teased. 'Cheers. And thank you very much. The food's keeping warm but we mustn't leave it too long. It smells delicious.'

'Buying you supper is the least I can do.'

She sat down opposite him. 'Jake brought your stuff as well. He says to tell you bad luck, and get fit soon so he can thrash you at tennis.'

Hal raised his glass to her. 'He's a nice young man. I can see the customers love him. When the bar's quiet we have a bit of a chat. I must seem a boring old fuddy-duddy to him, though.'

She refrained from enquiring into Hal's age. She reckoned he must be no more than two or three years older than she was. Fuddy-duddy he was not. Hastily, she blocked from her mind's eye certain images she wouldn't want Jake to know about.

Hal looked at her speculatively. 'Isn't this where you tell me I don't look a day over forty-five?'

'This wine is still beautifully chilled. You and I are probably much of an age, so I wouldn't dream of saying you were older than mid-to late-thirties.'

'Why, thank you ma'am,' said Hal. 'We males like that kind of comment too, you know.'

Zillah was about to relax against the settee cushions when she remembered the food. She put down her glass. 'Supper on a tray, I think. I won't be long.'

He groaned. 'I feel so useless.'

'Don't be silly. And whatever you do, please don't try to rush things.' She headed back to the kitchen.

He was left pondering her last remark. What things? Did she think he was trying to soften her up? Perhaps Zak had already made a play for her and been turned down. Or was she referring to the sprained ankle and its recovery time? Gloomily, he drank a little more wine. He was hardly in a position to chase Zillah down the garden path, should she have any fears in that direction. Although he wasn't yet forty, any able-bodied senior citizen could certainly out-walk him at the moment.

In any case, after overhearing her comment about not fancying him, he was hardly likely to launch a charm offensive, whether on crutches or not. Zillah had consigned what happened between them to the Deleted folder. At least this annoying accident of his seemed to have cleared the air, to the point where they could talk to one another like normal people.

He gave her his full attention when she served their dinner and he commented on another stunning picture, a seascape this time.

'I don't talk too much about Daniel, but oddly enough, today I bumped into someone who's been collecting some of his work. I have rather a lot of pictures stored in the spare room, and I know they'd fetch money if I managed the sale properly.'

'That's something I can't advise you upon, but I'm sure you know how to make the initial enquiries . . . '

'I do. But let's enjoy our dinner now. It's been a long day, for both of us.'

★ ★ ★

Next day, Zillah cooked a traditional Sunday lunch. Hal put down his knife and fork and sat back in his chair. 'That was the best meal I've eaten in a long time.'

'Why, thank you, but it's only a Sunday roast and trimmings.'

'Vegetables fresh from the garden? Mint sauce not from a bottle? It was wonderful, but I feel guilty about you cooking for me.'

She finished her glass of water. 'I don't often get to cook for two. It makes a nice change.'

'Well, it's much appreciated. What are you up to this afternoon?'

As Hal had noticed, they'd fallen into an easy sort of camaraderie. The initial hesitation had vanished as quickly as the delicious roast meal. They were talking about books and films and television programmes they liked. They both enjoyed watching tennis and rugby, and each of them hated Monopoly but loved Scrabble.

'If you don't mind being left alone, I think I'll walk into town. I want to check out the art galleries — see what kind of stuff is in the windows.' She bit her lower lip. 'I'm a bit out of touch with that kind of thing nowadays.'

311

Immediately, Hal wondered whether she'd reached too hasty a decision about selling any of her late husband's work, after their discussion the previous evening, but didn't want to intrude. Having now seen several stunning paintings by Daniel Robinson, he was curious as to why Zillah kept such a low profile. Surely by now it had occurred to her that she might be sitting on a considerable amount of money.

'Don't be so polite. You mustn't concern yourself about me,' he said. 'I only wish I could wash up for you.'

'Most of it's done,' she told him. 'I'm boringly organised in the kitchen.'

'Boring is the last word I'd use in connection with you,' he said softly.

Zillah pushed back her chair and got up. 'Let's make you comfortable on the settee.' Her tone reminded Hal of the eagle-eyed matron years before when he was at prep school.

14

Zillah returned from her stroll, still not sure how she felt about putting Daniel's pictures up for sale. She put her head round the sitting-room door to see if Hal needed anything, and saw he was lying on the settee, head propped on a cushion, feet buried beneath a heap of Sunday papers. She couldn't help smiling at the crowning touch — even though she wondered how the little cat had blagged her way in. Ruby was curled up on Hal's chest, cradled by his cupped hand.

Slumbering man and sleeping kitten were oblivious of her return. And Hal, despite his six feet three inches of professional manhood, had shed a couple of decades. A cheeky sunbeam highlighted a tiny auburn glint in his dark eyebrows and set Ruby's silvery fur gleaming. If only Daniel could be here, Zillah thought, he'd be sketching the pair of them, intent upon capturing Hal's vulnerability.

She left the sitting-room door ajar and went into the kitchen, where she shut herself in. The door through to the utility room was ajar, which had allowed Ruby to creep through the gap and find her way into yet another person's heart.

Zillah plunged her gloved hands into hot and foamy washing-up water to tackle the remaining dishes. She wished she could find the confidence to let herself love again. She'd always love Daniel. That was a given. But somehow that sitting-room tableau she witnessed had left a very large lump in her throat. It was difficult to imagine how she'd once found Hal arrogant and obnoxious. She scrubbed furiously at an obstinate stuck-on bit of roast potato, and tried not to think how lovely it had felt when he nuzzled her neck.

★　★　★

Monday morning, Zillah heard Hal clump his way along the hall to the bathroom after she'd showered and dressed. He'd insisted he could manage alone in there, and for that she was grateful. At least he could prop himself up at the washbasin to complete his ablutions in privacy. She met the invalid on his way back to his room, in a navy-blue towelling robe and a drift of spicy sandalwood.

'I'm off to work in a minute, Hal. Can I get you anything before I leave? Sure you'll be able to hop to the kitchen?'

He nodded. 'My ankle feels easier today.'

'All the more reason not to overdo things.'

'You're wearing your headmistress face,' he teased.

'I need to with you and Zak around. Not that he's here much at the moment.'

Hal's eyes narrowed. 'I expect you miss him.'

But Zillah didn't let herself be sidetracked. 'I've secured the door to the utility room. I don't want Ruby streaking in and sabotaging your crutches. She's a fast mover. We daren't risk you falling again.'

He groaned. 'At this rate, you'll have me feeling like your ancient great-uncle.'

Ooh, no. Not when he smelt so delicious. Not when his eyes gleamed with merriment and she'd a fair idea he was naked beneath that severe towelling robe. *Don't go there.*

'I'll bring your post if there's any,' she said. 'You'll find bread in the bin and food in the fridge. Try to stay horizontal as much as possible. Is your laptop still in the sitting-room?'

'It is. So I can at least catch up with some work. If you could bring my appointments diary back with you this evening, that'd be great. I think I've updated my computer calendar, but I should check.'

'You'd better give me your office keys, then.'

'They're on the chest of drawers in my room — Zak's room,' he corrected himself. 'It'll be quicker if you fetch them.'

* * *

As Zillah drove out of the city, she wondered how many sides there were to Hal. Yes, he had the capacity to be remote and difficult. He could also be friendly and, well, highly kissable. And now she found he kept his keys attached to a heavy copper chain announcing that it opened the gateway to Alcatraz. There existed a zany sense of humour he kept hidden far too much. She also wondered how long it would take before he was more mobile. Hal was probably hoping he could go straight back to his cottage rather than his room at Mickey's hostelry.

It was weird how she'd originally thought sharing with Zak would be fun. In reality, she found his barely-veiled admiration a little annoying. She had no idea why this should be. There was nothing remotely creepy about him, and most women would melt like chocolate in the sunshine if they had hunky Zak to sing for them. On one occasion, while they'd peeled vegetables together, he'd sung *My Eyes Adored You* in a pure caramel tenor voice. There was no pleasing some people. Now she was having a job keeping her hands off her accountant, a man who probably couldn't wait to escape from his prison wardress.

Mrs Robinson's 'Top Up Your Freezer' offer was going pretty well. There'd be three deliveries to make later, all of them to elderly customers in central Bath. If she timed it right, she could go straight home after making her calls. The next outside catering job was midweek — an intimate, no-expense-spared wedding celebration.

Zillah's spirits plummeted, realising how quiet the following week would be. While she halted to allow a lorry through a gap in the traffic, she realised she should think hard about her business's way forward. Very hard. At least there'd be Hal on tap to offer advice if necessary. She selected first gear, gave the lorry driver a wave, and drove on.

At just after nine, she unlocked her office to find the phone ringing, and almost tripped over a chair leg in her haste to get there.

'*Mrs Robinson*, how may I help you?'

'You can say your name again for me. Hearing your voice sends shivers down my spine.'

'I almost broke a leg trying to reach the phone, for goodness' sake! What do you want, Zak Silver?'

He sighed down the line. 'I want you. But I doubt very much I can have you. Speaking of damaged legs, have you been sitting on Mr Christmas's chilly lap, or do I still stand a chance?'

Oho — Zillah felt her cheeks warming. Thank goodness Zak couldn't see her blush like a schoolgirl. He might suspect she really did harbour romantic feelings towards Hal. 'He and I are becoming friends, I think. Anyway, what are you doing up at this hour?'

'I'm walking to the tube station. Going for my audition. My mate was away last night and I felt like hearing a friendly voice.'

'I guess that means all your London friends are still in the land of Nod?'

'There's no one I'd rather speak to than you. I care about you, Zillah.' His voice was a purr.

'Why, thank you, Zak. I care about you too. So, break an egg, or whatever it is I'm supposed to say!'

'Cheers. I'm up for a part in a musical show that's touring. Something didn't work out, and my agent put me up for it.'

'Well, I hope it works out for you.' Zillah consulted her watch. 'I have to go now, Zak. I can hear my right-hand woman arriving.'

'Ah, the lovely Abi. Say hi to her for me, and take care, babe.'

The buzz of whatever city road Zak

was walking along ceased. Zillah replaced the phone and wondered why Abi was late. Not that there was any great rush. She found her assistant staring into space as if the building might tumble around her — and if it did, what did she care?

'Do you want to tell me what's wrong?' Zillah kept her voice even.

Abi struggled with a sob. 'Joe. Us. It was horrible, Zillah. We had a row last night.'

Zillah resisted an urge to say, *Oh, is that all?!* It wasn't unknown for the couple to have the occasional tiff. 'You'll make it up later. You always do.' She gave Abi a hug. The girl clung to her.

'I don't think we'll make up this time. It was a biggie.'

'Not the M-word again?'

'Of course the M-word again. I do love Joe. You know I love Joe. He knows it too. I just don't want the whole marriage thing to swing into operation. Not yet. I like being us. As we are.'

'You'll still be you if you marry Joe,'

said Zillah softly. 'Have you ever thought he might be afraid of losing you?'

'But why would he be? He knows how I feel about him, even though I don't have a ring on my finger.' But Abi sounded a tad unsure.

'Please don't take this the wrong way, Abi. You're such a lovely, friendly person, he might fear some other man could get the wrong idea if there's no outward sign you're partnered. Some-one like Zak, for example, might well make a move. Of course, he knows you're spoken for.'

'I marked Zak's card the first time we met! Anyway, that guy has a huge crush on you.'

'He's an actor. He can't resist performing. Maybe Zak's not such a good example. He says to say hi, by the way,' Zillah added. 'Joe knows you mix with lots of people when you're at a function. What does he do with himself when you have to work Saturdays?'

'Sometimes he does a few chores.

Cooks something for us to eat later. Watches sport on telly. He might go and have a bite to eat with his mum and dad.'

'Hmm.' Zillah thought for a moment. 'He never goes to a party on his own or out for a drink?'

'He likes a beer or two with his squash partner after their Tuesday night game. That's when I catch up with chores. I'm always there when he gets home. He's always there when I get back from a function.'

Zillah suppressed a smile. 'Forgive me, Abi, but you two already seem like a married couple.'

For a moment Abi looked stunned. Then a slow smile spread over her face. 'Yeah, we do, don't we?'

'I think it's a good sign. Marriage is the cementing of a good relationship. You send out a statement of commitment to one another. You forge a bond.' Zillah's face softened. 'And one day, if you want children, you've got love and friendship plus mutual commitment as a base to go forward from.'

'Goodness,' said Abi. 'Sounds like you wish you could be married.'

Zillah's heart seemed to stutter, dipping and swooping like the gulls haunting the Cornish coastline. Abi was probably gasping for a coffee. Zillah's hands moved swiftly and competently while she struggled with her emotions. It was difficult when she was being teased by the image of a tall man with hair a deeper shade of golden syrup, plus broad shoulders made to cry upon. Guilt over her dawning love for Hal and her deep-seated love and sadness over Daniel made for a bittersweet emotion.

She saw the distraught expression on her young assistant's face.

'I'm so sorry, Zillah.' Abi shook her head. 'That was totally out of order. My tongue runs away with me sometimes.'

'Like it did last night?'

'I'm afraid so. I told Joe to stop hassling me. Said if he didn't, I'd definitely go out with some other guy, just to annoy him. I know I'm stupid,' she wailed. 'I didn't mean it, though. I wouldn't date anybody else, even if Zak asked me — and he's definitely eye-candy. If a tad old,' she added.

'Isn't he just!' said Zillah, loving the description. 'And so is Joe eye-candy. Plus he's far more dependable than Zak, and he loves you to bits. We all say things we don't mean sometimes. It's having the guts to admit it, then try and repair the damage caused, that's the hard part.'

She handed Abi a steaming mug. 'Come on. There's shortbread in the tin. We'll sit down and go through today's jobs. Drink your coffee and send Joe a text, why don't you? Tell him you love him. Tell him he's the only man in the world for you.'

'You're such a softie,' said Abi, her eyes sparkling again. 'You should become an agony aunt, Zillah. Make it part of the *Mrs Robinson* wedding package.'

Zillah remembered Cara Nancarrow, the lovely bride with cold feet to match her bridegroom's. How Cara had cried on her shoulder on her wedding day. 'Maybe it's easier to sort out other people's problems than my own.'

Abi's concentration appeared to be elsewhere, though her smile was serene. Her thumbs flew as she texted. When she put her phone down, it gave a knee-jerk beep. She grabbed it, almost knocking over her mug, which her boss hastily moved away from danger. It was worth it, thought Zillah, seeing the expression upon Abi's face as she read Joe's message.

★　★　★

Back at Zillah's flat, Hal was inserting his scalpel into *Mrs Robinson's* accounts. Zillah had begun a new trading period and he'd suggested taking a look at first soundings. He'd almost been tempted to leave the utility room door ajar, but his hostess's words rang in his ears. He certainly didn't want to risk further damage to his ankle. He wasn't normally a cat kind of person, but Ruby was something different. He loved the idea of her facing up to the other two 'divas', as Zillah described them. The kitten was a diversion. Not that he needed any such thing when Zillah was around. Hal's feelings, having fluctuated around the time of the cold war between them, were now firmly focused.

That first kiss was difficult to forget. As was the embarrassingly silent taxi ride back when he'd longed to take her hand and reassure her he had no intention of taking advantage of her having drunk a couple of glasses of wine. What happened after that still made him wonder if he'd been hallucinating.

But equally unforgettable were her words that day outside her office, when he'd arrived just in time to hear her describe to Abi just how much she wasn't attracted to him. That had hurt. Deeply. He'd been shocked at his reaction. If he hadn't realised it before, that was the moment when he knew he was in love with Mrs Robinson, for better or worse. Probably for worse, in Zillah's opinion.

Concentrate, man. Muttering, Hal moved to another item, frowned, and checked carefully before tapping numbers into the calculator. He'd advised her that a cash injection would help purchase another refrigeration unit, as well as keep on the straight and narrow regarding her bank loan. But there was a worrying trend apparent in the last weeks. The cash injection he'd suggested was beginning to appear not just advisable, but absolutely vital.

15

Zillah, looking forward to making supper for two again, wondered if Zak's arrival had triggered something she'd been burying. Being independent was one thing, constructing a barricade was quite another. Her mum had hinted as much, as had Abi. But it was all very well for onlookers to offer advice. The person in question needed to be the one deciding how to spend her life. And Zillah knew, having been partnered for seventeen years, that she badly missed the companionship, the everyday trivial things, woven into the fabric of marriage.

She knew Daniel wouldn't have expected her to stay on her own for the rest of her days. He'd told her as much one night, towards the end. She'd stopped his speech with a kiss, unwilling to contemplate the void underlying his poignant words. But those words came back to her now whilst her van ticked over in rush-hour traffic, as she stole glances at shoppers, sightseers and smartly-dressed businessmen and -women spilling across crowded pavements.

Considering her coastal upbringing, Zillah had adapted well to being a townie, despite exhaust fumes and hordes of chattering Continental teenagers soaking up culture. Bath was a multifaceted gem and she never tired of exploring its treasures, its parks and alleys and its specialist shops. Cornwall would always stir her blood but she could exist away from it, helped by so many reminders treasured in her late husband's vibrant depictions of sea storms, peaceful harbours and breathtaking skies.

At last she was on the move again, turning into her road and entering the driveway. Would Hal be pleased to see her or was she being presumptuous? She had a horror of rejection. It was one of the reasons why she hadn't begun dating. People seemed to think after you'd been widowed for a year or so, you should get out there again. It wasn't that easy. She was two decades beyond her eighteen-year-old self. Those girlish dreams and career plans had fizzled away in Daniel's charismatic presence, yet had been rekindled in a different way as she fell more and more deeply in love.

Yes, she had completed her cookery course. Everyone knew that was the right thing for her. But she hadn't achieved her full potential, nor had she much cared. Life had offered a new path, which she'd adored following with her gentle, dreamy artist husband. Trips abroad balanced peaceful days tucked up in their Cornish cottage with its inglenook fireplace. They'd walked, and risen early to swim together when the sea's temperature wouldn't freeze them to the bone. She'd continued to help in her parents' hotel, especially during busy periods. There were frequent trips to London and Bath in autumn and winter. Daniel would have understood her decision to relocate to one of their favourite cities.

Since being left on her own, she'd crafted a new and very different life for herself — one with more deadlines and dilemmas. Even at this stage, she sometimes checked her reflection in the mirror and wondered who that stranger in the smart suit was.

'You mustn't lose the plot now,' she whispered as she climbed out of the driving seat and locked the van. So her venture needed a financial boost? Maybe, just maybe, the answer was literally under her nose. Maybe it was time to lose sentimentality and accept practicality.

Zillah let herself in through the side gate. A silvery ball of fluff shot from the carrot patch and skidded to a halt beside her. She bent to pick up Ruby. It was cupboard love, for sure. Was that the reason why Hal was being so affable? Because he knew which side of his bread the jam was spread?

She entered the kitchen to find it empty. 'Hello,' she called.

'I'm in here.' His voice emanated from the sitting-room.

She headed down her hallway.

'I haven't moved from this spot since I collapsed here after breakfast.' He gave her an uncharacteristic wink.

She shot him one of her headmistress glares. 'With no coffee on tap? I don't think so, Mr Christmas.'

'I should have brewed up for you, but I wasn't sure when you'd be back.'

He sounded a little guarded. Zillah wondered what was going through his mind. Knowing her luck, her calculations probably weren't causing him too much joy.

'A cuppa would go down well,' she said. 'Give me a few minutes and you can join me.'

''You think I can do with the exercise?'

'I think you've got the *Mrs Robinson* folder beside you for a reason.' She locked gazes with him.

'We do need to talk. Yes.'

'Give me time to sort the cats out as well as brew tea.' She needed time to think. If he was about to give her unwelcome tidings, she needed to have a few questions ready, not to mention solutions.

★ ★ ★

'So you see what's happening? Your profit's taken a dive. Projected business is fairly good, but you definitely need to expand in other directions. The main wedding season isn't long enough to keep you in the black. And some of your smaller jobs aren't really worth the trouble.'

'I wonder what my elderly ladies who lunch would make of your comment. It really is that bad?'

'When we spoke before, you knew it wasn't a dream scenario. You've put certain measures in place, and that's good. But you need to be thinking big.'

'Additional equipment? I'm well aware of that. We talked about it before.'

'Indeed.' He picked up his cup. 'Forgive me, but I just wondered if you have any more of these wonderful paintings.' He gestured to the one over the fireplace. 'That is you, isn't it? Gazing out to sea?'

She nodded. 'A much younger me, of course. Daniel used it for exhibition purposes, but wouldn't sell. I told him he should — that sounds very conceited, but it's all about his interpretation of the model, whoever it is. Of course, he didn't listen.'

'I'm not surprised. There are some things you can't put a price on. And it's obvious how the artist felt about his beautiful sitter.'

Zillah remained silent.

'Don't look so startled. I may be a number-cruncher but that doesn't prevent me from appreciating raw talent when I see it. I've spent a lot of time on line today, researching your late husband's work,' said Hal. 'You do realise there are collectors avid to buy?'

She nodded. 'I've given it a great deal of thought lately.'

'In the small hours?'

'Sometimes. You know, Hal, I went through a stage where I couldn't bear to think of even going through Daniel's unsold paintings. They seemed kind of sacred. It was as if I'd be desecrating his memory.'

'I understand where you're coming from. Those paintings are a part of him, and they're very special to you for different reasons than the urge to complete a collection.'

Hal was watching Zillah carefully. She'd pulled out her hair slides so her silky locks fell either side of her face, screening her expression. He worried she might be tearful, until she raised her head again and he saw the determination in her eyes.

'Everything's clear to me now. Daniel didn't leave me a big pot of cash, apart from the equity in our cottage. But what he did provide was a legacy. I have a stash of paintings, their value as yet unknown, but definitely worth examining with a view to selling. In the grieving days, it didn't occur to me. He wasn't — well, we weren't materialistic people.'

'I understand. But the best and bravest thing you can do now, for yourself and in memory of Daniel, is to set aside the pieces you can't part with, and arrange for the remainder to be priced and exhibited with a view to sale. As quickly as possible.'

'And if I can raise sufficient cash, you feel *Mrs Robinson* is worth carrying on? I did tell you one of my competitors has stopped trading?'

'Yes, and that might mean a bigger piece of the pie for you, if you'll pardon the pun. Zillah, you're still building your business. Some of your bookings are with five-star clients. You need to be innovative and bold. Speculate to accumulate, as people always say.'

She got up. 'No pressure, then!'

Hal mimicked a pistol shape with his

hand and pointed it at her. 'You know you thrive on pressure, Mrs Robinson.'

'All right. I'm off to fix supper now.' She handed him the remote control. 'I expect you want to watch the news. All men like watching the news, don't they? Especially number-crunchers.'

★   ★   ★

For the first time in a while, Zillah slept straight through a dreamless night. This seemed to seal her decision to take Hal's advice, as she'd more or less reached the same conclusion anyway. That chance meeting at the golf club with Lionel had tripped a switch, forcing her to accept her position. Hal reckoned he could begin sorting the canvases and creating an index. He said it was another way of saying thank-you for her hospitality.

If Zak had volunteered to take on the task of cataloguing Daniel's pieces, she knew she'd have found some excuse to decline. Despite the rocky start to their relationship, if indeed it was such a thing, she trusted Hal utterly. She knew his financial advice made sense, and now she was entrusting him with her late husband's precious pictures. Perhaps she should mention that bundle of gold sitting there amongst the jumble of picture frames. A little voice sang in her ear: *What next? Will you, would you, ever consider trusting Hal with your heart?*

16

Next morning, parking in her usual space outside the premises, Zillah reminded herself of the importance to stop thinking of Hal in any way but realistically. He was a businessman. She was a businesswoman being helped to realise her assets. Anything beyond a totally professional relationship was unthinkable. She must be under no illusions over that.

'Oh no!' She pulled out her phone and rang Hal's mobile. In the morning dash she'd completely forgotten to ask him to watch out for the hidden jewellery.

'Sorry, Hal,' she said when he answered. 'I forgot to ask you to keep your eye open for a black leather pouch when you're going through the pictures. It contains some jewellery that belonged to my late mother-in-law, but I can't recall exactly where I packed it.'

She wrinkled her nose, listening to his reply. 'I know, I know. You're absolutely right. I promise to bring the whole lot into the office tomorrow and put it in the safe.'

★ ★ ★

At noon, Zillah was about to leave for an appointment. Abi was happily sculpting what she described as at least a ton of her beloved marzipan fancies, when the phone rang.

'Zillah? Annie West speaking.'

'I planned to ring you later this week, Annie. How are you getting on?'

'Minor crisis, I'm afraid. Not your department, but we wondered if you could help. My daughter's friend, the one due to sing at the church, has announced that she's pregnant.'

'How lovely for her. Or — ?'

'Of course, she and her husband are thrilled,' said Annie in her cut-glass tones. 'But she's been advised to take things very carefully. No more bookings for the foreseeable future.'

'I see. Do you have a replacement in mind?'

'Not a clue. Wouldn't know where to start. I wondered if you had any ideas.'

'Must you have a soprano? Could the singer be a tenor?'

'Gosh. Goodness. I don't see why not. Can't remember what song was chosen. Wouldn't be the end of the world if a chap did the job, I suppose.'

'I can recommend a fantastic tenor with masses of experience. He's versatile and reliable.' Zillah crossed the fingers of her free hand. 'Shall I see if he's available?'

'Would you? In the meantime, I'll get back to my daughter. Speak soon.'

Zillah checked her watch. She had time to make a quick call. Securing a booking for Zak would help her score brownie points with the West family, and it would be great for him and for Hal if he landed the gig and made a good job of it. The West clan had more good connections than the electricity board. She picked up the phone and, without thinking, selected her home number on speed dial.

* * *

Hal sat surrounded by big sky, the sea in quiet, calm mood, and the sea in fractious, frightening mood. In the harbour, boats bobbed, vivid gouts of colour on the water, while fishermen, their faces etched with loving care, unloaded their catches or mended their nets. Heaps of silver sardines gleamed from the canvas. He could almost smell the ocean.

There was Zillah again, like a barefoot gypsy girl on the beach, light silhouetting shapely legs beneath long, flimsy skirt. It was a Princess Diana moment, and Hal caught his breath at the loveliness of the model and the skill of the artist. The love shared by husband and wife must have been such that every time Daniel captured her

343

image, he discovered something new, something precious, each discovery clearly a delight.

Sometimes Hal laughed out loud, or whistled in appreciation, acknowledging the sheer magic of the painter. He knew the importance of light in art, but he'd never realised the extent of Robinson's genius.

He felt a pang of regret over Daniel's passing, both for his young widow and for his many admirers. He vaguely recalled the announcement of the artist's death on the radio — or maybe he'd skim-read the obituary in one of the broadsheet newspapers — but of course he'd never dreamt he might end up cataloguing so many stunning pictures. Even unframed and not properly displayed, it was obvious Zillah's blanket-wrapped legacy deserved the title of 'treasure trove'.

When he heard the phone in the hall ringing, he contemplated not answering what was probably a cold caller. Zillah wouldn't be getting in touch a second time; and even if she needed to, she'd surely ring his mobile again. The ringing continued. What if something had happened to her? If Abi was trying to get in touch, why didn't she ring his mobile number?

Stop being paranoid. Hal reached for his crutches, lost his balance and swayed like a tall tree in a gale. When he toppled, he landed a whisker away from the exquisite portrait of Zillah. Hal closed his eyes in relief as he realised he hadn't caused any damage, but the caller just wouldn't give up. Slowly, painfully and punctuated by groans and yelps, Hal used a dining chair to help him struggle upright.

This time he made proper contact with the crutches. No harm done. It must surely be Zillah calling him, because her friends and family would know she must be at work. She'd realise he needed ample time to stump down the hallway to the kitchen and pick up the phone. His hand was within an inch of the receiver when the ringing stopped.

Hal cursed softly beneath his breath, but had the presence of mind to punch 1471 and check who'd called. It was *Mrs Robinson*'s office number. Soon he heard it ringing and waited for Zillah to pick up. After what seemed ages, the answerphone kicked in, closely followed by the voice of a slightly breathless Abi.

'This is Hal Christmas, Abi. Was Zillah just ringing me?'

'Zillah? She's not here, Hal.'

Abi sounded so young and brimming with life, he thought. 'Someone just called the flat's landline from your number. I still can't fathom why she didn't ring my mobile.'

'I've no idea, but she could've been ringing you and gone out while I was still away from the kitchen. It's not like her to leave without telling me, though. How weird.'

'I imagine she had her reasons.'

'Maybe she forgot something. Do you want to leave a message?'

'Only that I returned her call. We

spoke earlier, which is why I'm a bit puzzled.'

'So, have you two managed to bury the hatchet?'

'Not in each other's heads, you'll be pleased to hear.'

Abi's giggle percolated down the line. 'I expect she enjoys your company. First Zak moves in and now you. Some girls get all the luck.'

'Or they draw the short straw,' he quipped.

The call ended, leaving Hal still wondering why Zillah might have rung without giving him time to answer.

★ ★ ★

She didn't often lose her temper. If she did, why did it always have to be Hal who irritated her? Driving back to the flat, Zillah was more worried than angry, but convinced herself she was cross with Hal for not being close to the phone where he should be. He'd got the hang of those crutches now and

347

should easily have reached it. Goodness knew, she'd rung for long enough. It could only mean he'd got into a pickle. Maybe he'd gone out for some fresh air. Driving away from the business park, she pictured him lying on the ground, unable to move because he'd damaged the other leg this time. Or worse.

'Come on, come on,' she muttered while waiting for the traffic lights to change colour. She had to check up on the wretched man to reassure herself he hadn't lost his balance and fallen, but she'd need to ring the bride's mother and apologise for running late. The date of this particular wedding was set for twelve months from now. Nothing awful would happen if her arrival should be delayed a little. Unless — ? *Oh no*, she thought. Not the hospital again, Hal, please.

What could he have been thinking of? Her fingers beat a tattoo on the steering wheel. A fracture on top of the existing sprain would set him back weeks, maybe months. The lights favoured her.

She turned off, heading for her driveway, where she cut the engine and jumped out of the van.

She unlocked the gate, banged it behind her and rushed towards her door. 'Hal?' She almost fell inside, shouting. 'Hal? Where are you?'

He was sitting at the kitchen table. He looked up at her and smiled. 'Hi. I assumed that must have been you, trying to ring me. What's up?'

Zillah blew up. She flung her keys on the table where they skidded, crashing into a slender vase of pink and mauve sweet peas. She put her hands on her hips and stood, glaring down at him. She hoped her eyes showed her anger because she was going to let rip right now.

'And you were right,' she said. 'I was ringing you, but where were you, Hal? I've been so worried. I had visions of you lying on the floor, unable to move. Concussed. Or worse. You're not supposed to take chances, you — you dunderhead.'

He was leaning back in his chair, a tiny smile playing on his lips. What, she wondered, was he up to?

'Even if you were in the bathroom, you could've got to the phone,' she raged. 'Do you have you any idea what I've been going through, worrying about you? Agonising over what might have happened! I rang for ages.' Her voice faltered. Why was he giving her that strange look?

She realised he was struggling to stand.

'What are you doing?' She reached out to help him.

'No, Zillah! I can manage on my own. I'm absolutely fine. Yes, I did lose my balance and ended up on the floor. Don't worry. I managed not to damage any of the paintings when I landed.'

Her anger dissolved in a trice. 'As if I'd blame you if you had.' She brushed away a tear.

She saw Hal catch his breath. 'You were worried. You rushed out of the office to come and check up on me. Why, Zillah?'

'Because — because I care about you, that's why. I know I shouldn't, but I do.'

He grabbed a chair back, supporting himself.

'Shall I pass your crutches?'

He sucked in air. 'Did you just say you cared about me, Zillah? Define 'care', please.'

She blinked hard. 'I think I — I love you, Hal Christmas.'

'Only think?' He inched his way towards her.

She didn't move. She couldn't move. 'I love you, Hal. I know you don't feel the same way, but you have to know. Because I'm not sure I can bear being under the same roof with you, feeling the way I do. Especially after what happened between us — '

He was close to her now. Really close. So close she felt dizzy.

'Damn my wonky ankle,' he said. 'Do you think, if I hold you, you could stop me from collapsing? Again.'

To her surprise she felt calm. Sure. Ready. 'I'm prepared to give it a try.'

She felt the warmth of his arms through her thin blouse. She wrapped her arms around him and to make absolutely sure, wedged one thigh against the table to support the pair of them. She tilted her chin upwards so he could gaze down into her eyes, and gazed back, suddenly and wonderfully fearless.

His arms tightened around her. 'I want to kiss you again because I love you too.'

'Even though you thought I was a witch when we first met?'

'And what about you? I distinctly heard you tell Abi you didn't fancy me. Not one little bit.'

Their mouths were a whisper apart.

'You shouldn't necessarily believe everything you hear,' she said. 'And I thought you were arrogant.'

'Shall we stop talking now?'

This time they kissed like lovers.

They kissed, not in a wine-giddy moment, but because each of them was realising a dream. Sweet. Tender. Romantic. Above all, passionate. Zillah stopped worrying about everything, and started accepting how important Hal had become to her.

When they stopped kissing, they still clung together.

'I should go to my appointment,' she murmured, nestling against him.

'But I need lots of tender loving care.' He kissed the top of her head.

'I'll have to grovel to the client.'

'As your accountant, I should advise you to put business first. But before you leave me collapsed in a quivering mass, can you tell me again what you just said? Not the grovelling bit.'

She nodded. 'I love you. I love you very much. Is that better?'

'Very much better.' He kissed the tip of her nose. 'Seriously, my knees feel shaky.'

'Mine too. Much too shaky to walk away from you.'

Hal managed to sit down. He pulled her on to his lap. 'You cannot imagine how much torture it's been, feeling the way I do.' He hugged her close.

'Oh, but I can. I absolutely can.'

Their lips met again.

When they'd laughed together and he'd brushed away her tears and she'd fussed about how his ankle wouldn't like her sitting on his lap and he'd ignored her comment, Hal remembered something he kept meaning to say. 'I hate to spoil the moment, but something's bugging me, darling. That jewellery pouch you mentioned — is there any chance you might have hidden it somewhere else? I've unwrapped every single picture and there's no sign of it.'

17

She slid from his lap, her mind a whirlpool of possibilities. 'Please, Hal, tell me you're joking.' She rested her hands on his shoulders, watching his face. 'But you're not, are you?'

He shook his head. 'I never joke about serious matters. Before we investigate further, could you possibly have made a mistake?'

She straightened up and puffed air through her lips. 'Anything's possible, I suppose, with all that was going on. Yet I know I packed the jewellery in my overnight case before leaving Cornwall, so it stayed with me in the car. The morning after I moved in here, I remember I unwrapped the outer covering of one of the portraits so I could tuck the pouch inside.'

'Have you any idea which portrait that might have been?'

She thought for a moment before shaking her head. 'I'm sorry, Hal. My mind's a blank on that one.'

He hauled himself to his feet and somewhat shakily held out his arms. 'Look, why not leave me to worry about it? I promise to check everything again in case I missed it the first time. I know you need to go to your appointment now.'

While he hugged her, Zillah heard his ringtone. 'That's your mobile. I'll pass it to you.'

'I don't recognise the number,' he said when she handed over the phone.

Zak's excited voice burst into the room. 'Hal, just using a mate's phone to say I got myself a part. It's a short tour and I start next Monday. Isn't it great? By the way, how're you doing?'

'Very, very badly. I think I need a full-time carer.' He winked at Zillah who rolled her eyes and made strange signs with her hands.

'You kidding me?' Zak asked. 'Mate, I'll have to come back to pick up some kit. I'm sorry to let Zillah down of course.'

'Hang on,' said Hal. He held his phone out to Zillah.

She shook her head. 'Ask him if he can sing at a big church wedding. It's in Bath and it's the first Saturday in September. Lots of VIPs.'

Hal relayed the message and listened, nodding, not once removing his gaze from her face.

'Okay, Zak, let me know if you want us to post your phone to you. I'm really pleased for you. We both are, but I have to go. Zillah's mislaid something rather valuable so forgive me if I cut this short.' He ended the call, disallowing further comment from Zak.

'Zillah, was that why you were ringing me earlier? To tell me about the wedding singer gig?'

'Yes. I suppose I must have been so frazzled, I just pressed the flat's number on speed dial. Imagine, if you'd picked up quickly, I'd have asked you to pass Zak that message and I wouldn't have come back here. You and me mightn't have happened.'

He cuddled her to him again. 'Oh yes, we would. I'd have exploded otherwise. But you must get off to work now.'

'Not until you kiss me one more time. I hate to say it, but if we don't find that jewellery, I suppose I'll have to contact the police.'

Hal kissed her and held her at arms' length. 'And the police will ask you to provide a list of people having had access to the property since you last set eyes on the stolen item.'

He didn't need to spell it out. Zillah broke away. 'I don't believe I can feel such unbelievable happiness and yet be so devastated at the same time. I have to put this out of my mind until tonight. I have to go meet my client.'

'Drive carefully. We'll speak later, and meanwhile, I'll search again.'

She walked to the door. 'The weird thing is, knowing I might have lost the wherewithal to keep my business afloat, just as I find something very precious.'

★ ★ ★

'Oh man,' Hal spoke out loud late afternoon while Zillah was in her bedroom, changing out of her city suit. Despite his searching, he hadn't come across the jewellery pouch; therefore, Zak's name would have to go on that suspects' register. He hoped his suspicions were wrong. If the singer really had been up to mischief, he would personally find him and rip the guy to pieces, damaged ankle or not.

When Zillah came into the sitting-room, he'd already begun writing down names.

'We need every single name you can think of. Everyone who's been inside this flat since you put the jewellery in with the paintings.'

'Surely not everyone, Hal? You wouldn't suspect my landlady, for example?'

He shook his head. 'No, but in

practical terms, no one should be left out, not even the honourable Clarissa. And try to remember the names in order of access.'

'I definitely don't need to mention the removal men.'

'As long as you're absolutely sure you packed the jewellery in your case and removed it after the men had gone.'

'I'm certain I didn't hide it until the next day. But in the first few weeks here, I found a few things that needed attention,' said Zillah. 'I didn't meet the guy who fixed the kitchen window catch because my landlady arranged that.'

'I'll write down 'window repairman'. I doubt she stood over him.'

'Someone came to inspect a damp wall.' Zillah was supporting Hal's feet on her lap. 'I was at home that time, but I didn't go round with him.' She sighed. 'I hate doing this. I'm not letting you put the gardener's name down. He's worked for Clarissa forever.'

'Sweetheart, I have to write down his

name and the damp inspector's, or it's not worth doing this. The police will need to know.

She frowned. 'All right: Gardener. Damp specialist. Heating engineer and, um — '

'What about reading the electricity meter? What happens?'

'Each flat's meter is in the front porch. So the meter man never comes down here.'

'Anyone else you can think of?'

'This is ridiculous,' said Zillah. 'These people are all trustworthy.'

'Don't think about that. Concentrate, Zillah.'

'I suppose I have to include my landlady's curtain lady. She's another one who's been around for a hundred years. Surely it's not necessary to put her on the suspects' list?'

Hal sighed. 'Try to stay calm, Zillah.'

'I am calm.'

'So, has anyone else been here? Any of the neighbours? Think very hard.'

Zillah thought. Began rubbing the

toes of Hal's good foot. 'I've shied away from socialising. So the only other person I can think of is Abi.'

'You do a great massage. Are you saying Abi's been here without you?'

'On one occasion only, and that was when I stupidly left an important letter on the hall table. Only remembered it when I was on the London train. I had to ring Abi and ask her to go round and collect it so she could post it. Obviously I rang Clarissa and told her Abi had my permission to borrow the spare key. This is pointless, Hal!'

He took her hand. 'You've almost done.'

She stared at him. 'You surely don't think — '

'I don't think anything. Zak's name needs to be on the list — and there's still one more person, of course.'

'Now you really are joking.'

'I'm writing my own name before Zak's, just in case we get as far as the police.'

Zillah bit her lip. 'If only I'd been

more careful. If only I'd put the jewellery in my office safe. You must think I have the IQ of a chickpea.'

Hal pulled her towards him and she snuggled alongside. 'You were under stress,' he said. 'This kind of thing happens. Except mislaying a bunch of valuable gold jewellery's not quite the same as having a box of paperbacks vanish.'

'I'll check everywhere I can think of, in case I'm mistaken. Informing the police has to be the absolute last resort.'

★ ★ ★

In London, Zak couldn't settle, having spoken to Hal. Now he stared at the parcel he planned to have couriered to the *Mrs Robinson* office. He'd chickened out when it came to having Zillah's gold jewellery valued; and, when he'd got this new job, he'd contemplated driving to Bath with the object of replacing the precious package before Zillah discovered its absence.

But he'd known Hal was still in residence and might suspect something.

The situation had changed now. Hal hadn't said as much, but Zak felt sure he'd meant the jewellery was what Zillah had mislaid, and he hated to think of her worrying herself sick over it. Damn it! He'd been such a fool. He'd tempted Fate and now suffered the backlash. He'd also learnt a lot about commitment and friendship in a short space of time. People had been kind to him, Zillah and Hal particularly — even though she was concerned about her missing package, she'd thought about him and given him the chance of another booking.

He thanked his lucky stars he'd come to his senses in time, but knew how much he risked by dealing with the matter in this way. Once the package arrived, he'd be dead meat. Zillah would be able to hand the police an easy pinch, even though Zak might protest he'd always had her best interests at heart. Hal would come down on him like an avalanche. Zillah had no business leaving such temptation unguarded, but could he really take the coward's way out?

18

Hal's mobile phone rang while Zillah was trying to get her head round the awfulness of having to contact the police. She stood up when he answered the call, but Hal waved to her to stay where she was after he heard Zak's voice.

'Hal, it's me. Please tell Zillah to stop worrying. I have her jewellery here.' He clenched his fist. 'I removed it from its hiding-place without her permission.'

'You what? Just what were you playing at?' Hal's voice would have sent a chill down an Eskimo's spine. 'Are you completely out of your mind, man?'

'I was curious as to what was in the pouch. When I found out, I couldn't believe anyone could leave a hoard like that so unprotected. I intended to have it valued for her, but I'm well aware I should be pole-axed.'

'Too right you should. Personally, I wish I could rip your stupid head from your shoulders.' He watched Zillah frown.

'Have you any idea how much upset you've caused? Zillah and I have turned the place upside down. Remember Zillah? She's the one who allowed you to stay in her flat. What the hell possessed you to go through her personal belongings?'

'I can only say how sorry I am.'

'Hold on.' Hal turned to Zillah. 'You've got the gist?'

She nodded.

'Do you want to speak to him? Are you considering action against him?'

'I just want my jewellery returned.'

'And you shall have it.' Hal resumed his conversation. 'Listen, Zak. You better get your ass in gear and come back here to apologise. It's up to Zillah to decide whether she needs to take any action over this. You've let her down badly, Zak. Let both of us down.'

'I understand that, and I can only

apologise from the bottom of my heart.'

'You're not playing the lovable bad boy now, Zak. Damn well do the right thing and return her property. Don't even think of sending it through the post, because you need to apologise to her in person. Afterwards, you can drive on to Bristol and reconcile with your father. Or else, like they say in the movies, you'll never work in this town again.'

* * *

The morning after his phone call, a very contrite Mr Silver arrived with Zillah's property plus a big bouquet of roses, Hal sat down with him in private while she put the flowers in water. She never knew what was said, but when Zak left, he promised to drive straight on to Bristol to visit his folks. Next day, Hal sent Zillah off to lodge the jewellery in a safe deposit box, for storage while she decided what she wanted to do with it.

Later that day, when she rang to break her good news to her parents, she suspected they were relieved — not only that she'd found someone to love, but also found someone who loved her back and respected Daniel's memory. She kept the unfortunate affair of the jewellery to herself. Hal had growled and stormed and growled again, but at last she'd persuaded him she had no intention of reporting Zak or removing the singer's link on the *Mrs Robinson* website.

Clarissa was crestfallen when she returned from her travels and received two months' notice from her best tenant. But Zillah assured her landlady she'd stay in touch, and would still be prepared to come round to feed the divas if no one else was available. And it was obvious Clarissa approved of Hal, too. Zillah hid a smile when she introduced him and the sherry bottle made an appearance.

Wedding breakfasts were sprinkled like confetti over Zillah's bookings diary for the next eighteen months; largely due, she felt, to the successful wedding reception on Brassknocker Hill. The West nuptials had gone not merely according to plan, but in true Bollywood style. Beautiful saris in brilliant saffron, turquoise, scarlet and jade drifted like exotic birds among the grey morning dress and pastel silks worn by many of the guests.

The repentant Zak's exquisite singing moved most people to tears, and even the starchier ones were left misty-eyed. Zillah's scrumptious food resulted in a flood of enquiries.

'However does he manage to chat up so many women at once?' Zillah felt bewildered after Annie West's goddaughter Chloe whispered to her how Zak had told her she was the most stunning bridesmaid he'd ever set eyes upon. Zillah suspected he'd said precisely the same thing to the three other attendants.

Abi proposed to Joe the morning after the West nuptials. The younger couple's wedding was planned for the autumn, and even Hal didn't frown at Zillah when she decided to give Abi a suitably low-key but stylish buffet reception. Zak had promised to come back and sing at the ceremony, even though he'd be performing in the West End by then.

★ ★ ★

In late autumn, Daniel's paintings went on sale. By this time, Zillah had moved into Hal's transformed cottage, and they were both at the London gallery for the opening night. She introduced Hal to Lionel, who expressed delight both at her new happiness and at securing three Cornish harbour scenes he'd long coveted.

Hal was chatting to Lionel's wife, but keeping Zillah in view, when he noticed the latter stiffen. She'd spotted the red Sold sticker on the frame of the oil painting of herself on the beach, her hands cradling a perfect shell. He knew she was finding difficulty in holding back her tears.

At once he excused himself and hurried to her side. 'I knew that one would sell quickly.' He put an arm around her shoulders and hugged her to him.

'Oh, Hal. Darling, I'm sorry. Yes, I know it's all for the best — all for the business, but — '

He could feel the tension fizzling in the air. People within earshot were glancing uneasily at one another. And why shouldn't they? Several of them had known Daniel Robinson personally, so realised what a wrench this must be for his young widow. Hal produced a snowy linen handkerchief. While Zillah's face was buried in it, he whispered something in her ear.

She emerged from the handkerchief, eyes wide. 'You've done what?'

'I've bought that picture for your wedding present. That one and maybe two or three others.'

People were moving closer but Hal

didn't move a muscle.

'I'm getting married?' Zillah's voice rang out in the sudden hush.

'You certainly are. If you'll have me, of course.'

'Why not ask and see?'

Hal dropped to one knee. 'Will you marry me, Zillah?'

'Yes. Yes, Hal, I will.'

People were clapping. Lionel's wife was wiping her eyes.

'I so hope Daniel would approve,' said Hal. He took both Zillah's hands in his and raised them to his lips.

'I know he would. I'm so fortunate to have this second chance of happiness. I love you, Mr Hal Christmas.'

He stood up again. 'There's something else I need to ask you.'

'Try me.' She held her breath.

'Tell me you won't steal my business name.'

DANGER IN PARIS

Ken Preston

Fearing their marriage is dying, Beth follows vague, inattentive Dan on his business trip to Paris, hoping to surprise him. But the surprise is on her when she discovers that Dan has been living a secret life that she never once suspected. As she finds herself plunged into a terrifying world of guns and cat-and-mouse pursuits, Beth's only companion is a husband who, following a car crash, can no longer remember anything about her, their children, what he does for a living, or even who they can trust . . .

A SONG ON THE JUKEBOX

Pat Posner

Polly has fallen head over heels in love with James Dean-lookalike, skiffle-playing Johnny — whom her mum has judged to be completely unsuitable boyfriend material. When Mum sends Polly to live with Gran in an attempt to split them up, Polly is determined to remain true to Johnny. Will Gran, like Mum, forbid her to see him? And what happened in the past to cause the discord between her grandmother and mother? Polly sets out to discover the truth, and the consequences are surprising.

THE TOUCH OF THISTLEDOWN

Rebecca Bennett

When Clare, a recently qualified solicitor, meets Neal on the way to her cousin's wedding in Suffolk, his arrogant views on a woman's place in the profession annoy her. Nevertheless, she finds herself reluctantly becoming very attracted to him, despite her involvement with a married partner in the firm where she works. Suffolk and Neal are never far from her life — or her heart; though when one of her clients makes an unexpected, desperate move, Clare finds she is fighting for her life as well as her future happiness.

LOVE AMONG THE ARTS

Margaret Mounsdon

When Stella Bates arrives at Minster House to take on the position of companion to the injured Lady Pamela Loates, she expects to live quietly in an outbuilding and focus on her photography. Soon, however, she finds herself looking after the two recalcitrant teenagers in the family, and it isn't long before the boorish attitude of Pamela's handsome son Rory softens into affection, and then love. But how long can Stella stay at Minster House, especially when she is being stalked by the sinister Buttonhole Man?